LADY JOE

LADY JOE

Mark Saha

The author may be reached for inquiries about rights and permissions
at sahamark735@gmail.com

ISBN: 1511865431
ISBN 13: 9781511865432
Library of Congress Control Number: 2015906714
CreateSpace Independent Publishing Platform
North Charleston, South Carolina

For Brigitta Gerke

ACKNOWLEDGMENTS

I am indebted to Sandra Smith and all the gifted writers of Write Away for their unwavering support and guidance, and to Johnell Martinez Shepard, Saul Isler, Daryl Henry, George Crowder, Liz Villasenor, and David Rudnick for reading the manuscript and offering valuable suggestions. I also wish to thank cutters across the country, who somehow found time to respond to my many questions; especially Adam Conrad, Danielle Des Lauriers, Megan Mowery, and Sophie Petersen. The cutters who spent much time with me at cuttings must remain nameless because we were too busy talking about horses to introduce ourselves. Finally, a very special thanks to Sally Harrison and James Bankston for their inspiration and encouragement. Ms. Harrison's *Cutting: A Guide for the Non-Pro Competitor* was my introduction to the sport some years back and remains unsurpassed.

Mark Saha

Jimmy's *Cornbread Thinks* column in *Quarter Horse News* never fails to astonish, delight, and enlighten me.

Any faults in this little book are entirely due to my own limitations.

CONTENTS

CHAPTER 1
THE BOYS

Something real bad had happened over at the Walker place. Lee Estes was in charge while everybody else was away, and when he tried to fix the trouble, things broke loose in a gallop to hell. It was a bizarre turn for the worse, and he realized nobody else in the world could save him now except Jim Harrison's wife.

Lee drove up to San Luis Obispo, where Jim worked the morning shift at the Angus Annie restaurant, and begged him to talk to Francine. Jim went pale when he heard what happened but said he was having marriage trouble and it was a bad time to approach his wife about something like this. Lee refused to leave and waited at an empty table with a glass of water until Jim's shift ended.

They took the shortcut across a vacant lot behind the restaurant to the unpaved, treelined street where Jim lived on the outskirts of town. Lee was lankier and easily kept up no matter how fast Jim walked, and his long hair flopped across his face as they talked. Jim had to get a haircut to work at the restaurant and was not allowed to wear boots and jeans to work like Lee. The boys had been tight since high school, and Lee urged him to reconsider his decision.

Jim shook his head in despair. "I can't ask Francine to do that, Lee. I just can't!"

"Jimbo, I've messed up a few times, but nothing like this. This is huge. Wade Sanchez is going to drop dead of a heart attack when he finds out. My pop said he would shoot me if I let Mr. Walker down."

"It's pretty bad. But I don't see what you expect me to do."

"You need to put it to her."

"She won't go for it."

"Remind her I was best man at your wedding."

Jim was not reassured.

"Well, just take a pistol and shoot me then," Lee said.

Jim shook his head again. "We'll have to think of something else."

"Can I say something as a friend? It's pitiful the way that you let that girl push you around. Stand up to her! Women respect that."

"Look, it's not a good time."

"Why? What did you do?"

"Nothing! Things are a little touchy right now. She'll get past it."

Lee had dated Francine in high school and knew about that part. "I hear you," he said, nodding. "Okay, I can appreciate that." He thought for a moment. "Well, let's make up a story then."

"I'm not going to lie to my wife!"

"No, no. I said a story. We'll tell her it's a business proposition. I'll say I'm pulling you in as my partner."

Jim was doubtful. "That's kind of a stretch."

Lee heaved a breath in dismay. "I'm flat up against it here, old buddy. Walker's got a buyer flying in from Dallas as we speak."

"Lee, I'm worried sick Francine is going to quit me."

"You're always saying that! She'd have gone a long time ago if she wanted that."

"Well, I'm sure not going to bring up something like this—not now. She can tell before I open my mouth if she won't like what I'm about to say."

"All right. Then let me do the talking. I can handle Francine. I know how to explain things so she'll go along with them. All I need is for you to hand off the ball. Will you do that for me, amigo?"

"Lee, you are scaring me to death."

"Let me run with it, compadre."

Lee's confidence was flying high. All he needed was for Jim to slip a foot in the door for him. Jim was not sanguine.

The boys had grown up near each other, and Lee had been getting into fixes like this for as long as Jim had known him. Once, back in high school, Lee's father had given him an old pistol that he did not want anymore. Lee filed off the disconnector so it would fire the entire clip when you pulled the trigger. They had a lot of fun shooting tin cans with it and watching them fly to pieces. Then, one day, Lee's father went and got it to kill a rat. The blast knocked him backward to land on the concrete floor while the clip blew out a wall of the garage. He was shaking so bad, Lee's mom had to take him to the doctor to get him calmed down. Lee swore to them he did not know what was wrong with the pistol. His mother made him throw it out.

Meanwhile, Jim was a good kid who had only seen the inside of a jail once, and that was with Lee. This happened in high school too, when Lee's scrapes had him pretty much on a first-name basis with police. Lee was in a hurry to get somewhere and took a corner too fast, rear-ending a car driven by an old lady who had stopped to drop off a passenger. Lee was in his old man's pickup without permission and with a suspended license, so he shoved the stick into reverse and took off. His folks worked during the day, so he swung the truck around the house and into the backyard. Jim had to hurry over and help pound a dent out of the bumper. They were hammering away at this when two police officers walked around the side of the house.

"Hello, boys," one said.

"Hey, Bill, Tom!" Lee greeted them with forced cheerfulness. "What're you up to on this fine day, Officers?"

"We were driving past and heard all this racket back here. Thought we'd see what's going on."

"Not much. Me and Jim are trying to bang a dent out of this bumper."

The officers exchanged a grin. "Well, Lee," one told him, "while you're about it, might as well put this back on there too." He handed Lee the front license plate, which had come off at the accident scene.

Though Jim had not been with Lee in the truck, he was taken to the police station too to get it all sorted out. Jim's folks had to come get him out of jail and did not want him hanging out with Lee after that. But the boys went to school together, so Jim's parents couldn't do a whole lot about it.

Lee had a gift for talking to the girls. He could walk up to a group of them and have them laughing and making casual conversation in minutes. He had dated most of the ones at school, but usually the relationships did not last long. Francine he dated for almost a year. Jim was secretly crazy about her but too scared to say much to her.

The three of them owned horses in high school and went to a lot of weekend cuttings. Jim was good at picking cows, and that impressed Francine. They came to know each other pretty well by the time she and Lee broke up. Lee did not mind when Jim and Francine began dating, because he was hustling other girls anyway. Francine had sensed Jim was crazy about her, and after a year with Lee, she appreciated a more reliable boyfriend.

Shortly after high school, they got married.

Five years after graduation, Jim still could not believe his blind luck in being married to Francine. He was worried that he would not be able to hold on to such a smart and attractive girl. She had studied to become a paralegal, found a promising position with a small but prestigious firm specializing in equine law, and was seriously considering going back to school for a law degree.

Not much had happened for Jim and Lee. They were good together working with cutting horses, but neither could afford such expensive animals after moving from home, so they no longer pursued this. Jim had at least worked himself up to assistant manager at the restaurant. Other than that, they did some hunting in season, went on overnight fishing trips, shot pool in a local beer hall, and watched a lot of sports on television. Francine felt that neither of them had moved on since high school and was aggravated that her husband wasted so much time with Lee.

Mr. Walker was an old friend of Lee's dad and offered to straighten the boy out. Walker took Lee on at his quarter horse ranch near Ojai to teach him the business from the ground up and make a man of him. Lee and Jim had always loved working with horses, and at some point Lee hoped to bring Jim into the Walker operation. But first Lee had to make good. He did not mind washing horses, mucking out their stalls, polishing tack, unloading hay, and other everyday tasks. Much of his time was spent exercising horses in the round pen for trainers.

Presently, Lee had a pretty good fix on the run of the place. Walker was in the movie business and might be away on a shoot for several months, and his trainers were often on the road with their helpers, showing horses at competitions. During those times, Lee supervised the unskilled help and was in charge of the everyday operations of the property. A house staff looked after the luxurious, sprawling ranch house.

Jim knew Francine was not going to be happy to find Lee back and in desperate need of her help. It was about the worst time for Jim to show up with him. But Jim knew that he needed to help Lee, no matter what. They had grown up together and would always be close friends. Girls, even wives, might come and go, but Jim knew Lee would always be there for him. If Francine were to quit on him, Lee would help him get though that somehow.

Jim and Francine rented a modest wood-frame house with an old-fashioned front porch and a squeaky screen door. There was sufficient yard in back for a pasture and paddock, where local zoning laws permitted them to stable her cutting horse, Mary Jane.

Jim looked as jumpy as a rabbit as they approached the house. He was pretty sure this was not going to fly.

CHAPTER 2

FRANCINE

Saturday morning was house-cleaning day at the Harrison household, and Francine was fighting an old vacuum cleaner that did not much want to suck dirt out of the living room carpet. She was a pretty girl with her hair up in a babushka and was wearing one of Jim's old dress shirts over cutoff jeans.

The boys waved to her as they mounted the porch steps. "Look who I found," Jim announced with forced cheerfulness as they passed through the screen door.

"Hey, girl!" Lee grinned from under the hair flopped across his face.

Francine did not look pleased to see her husband hanging out with Lee again. "Lee, what on earth are you doing up here this time of day?"

"Oh, just passing by."

They were shouting over the noise of the vacuum cleaner, so she shut it off.

"I happened to be out this way, and wouldn't feel right if I didn't say hello," he said.

"Do you still have a job?"

"Oh, sure! Still with the Walker outfit. Actually I'm pretty much in charge now."

"Somebody put you in charge of what?"

"Well, the whole shot. Mr. Walker's in Europe shooting a picture, and Wade Sanchez and the trainers are on the road showing horses. I supervise the ranch and look after the horses."

Francine was skeptical. "It doesn't look to me like you're doing a whole lot of supervising. Shouldn't you be down there?"

"Well, something important has come up. It's a business matter, and I need to get on top of it."

Jim looked uncomfortable. Francine sensed something was not right. "What kind of business?" she asked.

"Lee needs to borrow your horse," Jim blurted out.

"Don't tell her that!" Lee shot Jim an annoyed look. "Francine, he didn't explain it right. Jimbo, I said to let me do the talking."

"Mary Jane's not going anywhere," she said flatly. "I guarantee you that right now."

"Francine, a business opportunity has come up, and I'm trying to pull Jim in on it."

She gave her husband an accusing look. "You're going into business with Lee?"

"Well, I...I...I'd have to look into it."

"We're going to have us a little talk tonight."

"I know it." Jim nodded quickly, looking at his feet.

"Will you hear me out?" Lee said.

"I have to work today. We have a court appearance on Monday, and we'll be in preparation all weekend."

"Listen to me, girl. It won't take a minute."

She had gone to many weekend cuttings and shot a lot of pool with these two, and those had been fun days. But that was a while back, and it seemed to her that neither of the boys would ever grow past that. She sighed, clearly aggravated with them.

"Sit down while I finish this."

She turned on the vacuum again and fought with the stubborn old machine as it gripped the chewed-up carpet. The boys sat on the couch and watched. They had remarked since high school how much hotter she looked when she was mad about something, and house chores always put her out of sorts. Presently, she was done. A deafening silence fell when she shut off the machine, and light dust settled from the air as she pulled the vacuum apart and threw it into a closet.

Lee thought she was ready to talk, but just as he opened his mouth to say something, she walked out of the room. They sat and looked at each other while she got ready for work. They could hear water running for the shower, followed by the rattle of clothes hangers when she selected clothes from the bedroom closet and a clatter of cosmetic bottles while she put on her face at a mirror. Lee sat forward on the couch and stared into space, while Jim slouched back deep into it and studied his feet.

Francine returned as a stunning young legal professional in a slightly flouncy red dress with matching shoes. She had bound her flowing blond hair with a jet-black hair band that made Jim a little crazy. He could scarcely believe he was married to this girl, and it scared him to see how sophisticated she had become since joining a law firm.

Francine sat facing them in an easy chair and crossed her legs like a venture capitalist seeing a couple of entrepreneurs in need of start-up money.

"Okay, Lee, let's hear your proposition."

"It's like this, Francine. Mr. Walker has a wealthy client flying in from Dallas to stay at the ranch a few days. I'm supposed to pick him up at the airport and keep him entertained. I hear he's a top criminal defense attorney—that part might interest you. Anyway, he called and said to enter a blue roan mare into a local cutting while he's out here. He wants to take some action pictures of her to show folks back home."

"Why a blue roan mare?"

"I guess he likes them."

"Can't you ride Lady Joe?"

"The boys have got her out on the road," Lee said, lying his ass off to Francine.

"You work on a cutting horse ranch and can't come up with a blue roan mare?"

"Oh, sure! Actually went out and bought one out of my own pocket just yesterday, to make everybody happy. A mare called Spooks; got the papers right here. Pretty little nag, and fella said she could cut, so I entered her in Paso tomorrow. Trouble is, this morning I run a few cows past her and don't believe she's ever seen one before. She's just an ordinary saddle horse."

"And you want me to let you ride Mary Jane."

"Francine, I would be ever so grateful."

"Jim, are you part of this?"

"I don't know," he said quickly, almost jumping out of his skin. He looked out a window to avoid her stare.

"Why is any of this not adding up for me?"

"Francine, I'm desperate here," Lee begged. "Mr. Walker only hired me as a favor to my old man. Pops said he would shoot me if I mess this up."

"Jim, you and me are really going to have a talk tonight."

"I know it." Jim nodded quickly.

She studied them with a skeptical look. "Which one of you is going to tell me what's really going on here?"

"Nothing's going on," Lee insisted.

"Is this man thinking about buying Spooks?"

"He might," Lee said, "if he likes her. She'd make a good saddle horse for his kids. But it's not like she's a cutter or anything."

"And did you tell him that you intend to ride Mary Jane in her place tomorrow?"

"He won't care about that," Lee said. "He just wants some pictures for his wall."

Francine rose up from the chair. "My God, are we going to talk tonight!" she said to Jim, who was withering fast now.

"I'll tell him!" Lee said. "We're picking him up at the airport this afternoon and, swear to God, I'll explain that to him the minute he steps foot in California. Jimbo will be my witness."

She shook her head in despair. "Lee, you are giving me a headache, and I have to work today."

"Girl, I swear to God the man won't care. He just wants some pictures."

"And how is that a business proposition?"

"Well, I need Jimbo to pick cows for me tomorrow so Mary Jane can show plenty of action. He's an important client. If we make him happy, Walker could move me up into showing horses and working with buyers. Nobody picks cows like Jim—horses is what we know best. I'll pull him in as my partner. We might finally get something going. There's a lot of money in horses if you've got connections."

That was the first thing Lee had said that made sense. Francine honestly wanted to see these two get somewhere in life. But she still did not like it.

"I could get kicked out of the association for letting you ride Mary Jane under another horse's papers."

"Look at me, girl. Nobody is ever going to know."

"A scandal like that would reflect on the integrity of the law firm. They'd have to let me go."

"My pop will shoot me if you won't do this. Anyway, it's a good opportunity for Jim."

"Jim, is this something you really want, or are you just going along with Lee?"

"I think we should help him out, sugar."

"Don't call me sugar."

"Francine, I am crawling across the floor, begging," Lee added.

She put a hand over her eyes. "There's something the matter with me," she said. "Lee, why is it that every time you open your mouth, I end up talked into something headed south? I should ask a doctor if they have pills for this."

The boys watched as she stood very still for a moment with a hand over her eyes. Finally, she lowered the hand and shook her head.

"Well, let's see what Mary Jane has to say about this," she said with a sigh.

CHAPTER 3

MARY JANE

Mary Jane was grazing lazily across pasture under a blue Pacific sky along the foothills of California's coastal mountains. Lee followed Francine out the back door. She got a halter and lead rope from the tack room and handed them to him. Jim watched from the kitchen door to see what was going to happen. The blue roan mare looked up as they approached and then came over to Francine.

"Mary Jane, do you remember Lee?" she said fondly. "He wants to play. Would you like to play with Lee?"

"Why, hello there, lady friend," Lee said.

Mary Jane was not much interested in Lee but did not seem to mind him either.

Both boys knew how to let a horse get to know them. Lee held out his hand and allowed Mary Jane to sniff it, and then he stroked the bridge of her nose with it and moved it down across her cheek. "Oh, what a pretty girl you are," he whispered softly. He stroked her neck a couple times and then ran a reassuring hand along her back. "Oh my, look at you. What a fine lady!" Lee was careful to keep one hand on her at all times while looking her over so she would know where he was when she couldn't see him. "You are one sweet blue lady, for sure," he said. "My goodness!"

Back in high school, Francine used to make out like crazy with Lee in parked cars, and it annoyed her to see him win over Mary Jane with vaguely familiar moves.

"Pick it up, Lee," she said. "I have to get to work."

Lee slipped on the halter, and they walked her to the tack room. Francine watched while he saddled and cinched up the mare. She took the bit from him without any trouble. Lee briefly reassured her again and then positioned a foot in a stirrup and grabbed the saddle horn. Jim was still looking out the kitchen door to see if this would work. Most people can soft-talk a good-natured mare, but how she takes to them sitting on her is less predictable.

Lee swung up into the saddle as naturally as turning a doorknob to enter a room. Mary Jane reacted a little by throwing her head up with her mouth clamped tightly shut, but Lee just patted her neck again. She widened her stance to adjust for this new rider, who was forty or so pounds heavier than Francine. Lee sat on her for a moment and nothing happened, so it looked like she was all right with this part too.

Now Lee motioned for her to move. She was less sure about this; she cocked an ear and tilted her head to look back at him with one eye. He seemed to know his business, so she trusted him enough to move out into pasture, where they proceeded to take each other's measure. They broke into a little trot, but when Lee tried to pull up, she bucked. It wasn't much, but he had not expected it and lost a stirrup, so he tucked and rolled, unhurt, to the ground. Mary Jane waited patiently for him to get to his feet and recover his dignity. She did not object when he climbed back into the saddle.

"Don't pull back so hard," Francine called. "Just use a few short tugs."

"We're all right," Lee replied grudgingly.

Mary Jane seemed a little more tolerant now that she had spoken her piece. She sensed that Lee knew his business; he was light on the reins and gentle with leg pressure, communicating what he wanted with unambiguous confidence. If he should go a little too high on the reins or do something else she didn't like, she would let him know with a swish of the tail or by suddenly raising her head. Lee was quick to notice that and correct whatever had upset her.

After a little of this give and take, Mary Jane noticeably began to relax, and during a pause in the action she lowered her head to readjust the bit. She was somewhat satisfied that Lee would not do something crazy and was more willing to accept his cues. He carefully took her through a few turns; she was a smaller horse with less distance to cover and executed them smartly. Then he backed her up and finally sprinted her to a hard stop.

"She backs up really well," he remarked.

Lee trotted her back to the tack room, where he dismounted and began uncinching the saddle. "I wish there was time to run a few cows past her, but I think we'll get along just fine," he said.

"You should probably make your deep cut first," Francine said.

"How so?"

"You want to make it before she gets too excited. Mary Jane is a little full of herself. Once she shuts down a cow, she's so proud of herself that sometimes she has to celebrate."

"Celebrate?"

Francine snuggled up nose-to-nose with the mare. "My little baby is so proud of herself, aren't you, sweetheart? Yes, you are! Oh yes, you are!" She shook her head vigorously while nose-to-nose and went into a burst of baby talk.

The way girls carried on about their horses embarrassed Lee sometimes. "I can go deep on the first cut," he mumbled, pulling off the saddle. Jim came over from the house to help him with the tack.

"I'll be in the office all weekend, so I'm holding you two responsible for her."

"Francine, I swear, I owe you for the rest of my life," Lee said.

"I hope so. Do you need anything else?"

Lee shot a look at Jim, who shuffled awkwardly. "Actually, Francine…"

"What?" She turned on him with a hard look.

"The thing is"—Jim stumbled with embarrassment—"this came up so quick. Lee had to enter late at Paso and"—he took a breath—"we need five hundred dollars for fresh cows."

Francine looked at them.

"We have to show Pederson some good action," Lee jumped in. "Mary Jane won't be able to do much with cows that have already been worked."

Francine pondered this in silence. Abruptly, she turned and disappeared into the house. The boys exchanged a look, unsure what that meant. Jim crept into the house to see what she was doing. Francine was at their bill-paying desk, writing a check from their ledger. He retreated outside and nodded to Lee that they had fresh cows.

She returned shortly, waving the check in the air to dry the ink, and then handed it to Jim.

"We'll talk tonight," she told him.

Jim nodded silently.

"Is there anything else?"

"No, we're good, Francine," Lee said. "Jim is coming to the airport with me to meet Mr. Pederson, but I'll have him home early."

"I have to run," she told Jim. "Will you put away the tack before you leave?"

"We'll take care of it," he assured her. "You go ahead, sugar."

They watched Francine get in her car and leave.

"Jimbo, I believe this kite is going to fly," Lee mused.

CHAPTER 4
LADY JOE

The boys returned to the restaurant parking lot for Lee's truck and pulled onto 101 South to the Santa Barbara airport. They had to meet the Dallas attorney arriving on a commuter flight from LAX.

Lee suggested that Jim bring his cowboy hat to look more horse-savvy. Jim slid low in the shotgun seat of the pickup and pulled the hat over his eyes; he wanted things dark so he wouldn't be scared to death about what they were about to do.

"Okay, Lee," he said from the darkness under his hat. "Tell me about it. I need to hear how you managed to lose a first-class cutting horse like Lady Joe."

"I had some bad luck, Jimbo."

"Oh, okay. Yes, I heard of a fellow lost his lawn mower that way." Jim chuckled.

"Horses go missing a lot," Lee mumbled.

"Well, I'd say you took misplacing them to a whole new level."

"The situation got out from under me. She was gone before I knew it."

"Hey, I'm not rubbing it in or anything. I'm just curious how something like that is even possible."

Lee sighed. "Here I am, in charge while the trainers are on the road. Walker calls from Switzerland to say some Dallas attorney wants to pay four hundred thousand dollars for Lady Joe. This fellow told Walker to just pick a number out of the air because he wanted that horse. Walker said for me to wash and groom her then pick up the fellow at the airport and let him look her over. They're going to execute payment by wire transfer. Then I surrender the papers on her, and the fellow will hire somebody to haul her back to Dallas."

"I never heard of a sale like that before."

"It's crazy, Jimmy. The way I understand it, this Pederson isn't even a horse person."

"Lady Joe is a fine animal, but that price is way out of her league," Jim said.

"She had a pretty good run for a few years," Lee admitted. "But Walker is showing younger horses now. Probably nobody ever made an offer on her because she has some funny habits. That's why he jumped at this. He said to get all over it while money is on the table."

"So what did you do?"

"Well, I got on it, like he said. Brought her in from pasture to wash and groom her."

"Did you tie her off right?"

"Oh, hell, Jim! I know how to wash a horse. She loved every minute of it. I lathered her up with a real nice shampoo and then washed her down and ran the water out of her coat with a squeegee. She was so pretty and proud of herself. I tell you, she is still one fine-looking champion. Anyway, it was such a nice sunny day, I decided to take her on a little bareback run to dry her off."

"Oh, boy," Jim said, adjusting his hat.

"She really wanted to go, so I didn't see the harm. My jeans were a little wet, but I was feeling that horse under me, and with the wind and sun in my face—it was just good to be alive. I took her up into the foothills to see the ocean. Right then out of nowhere, a damned mule deer lit off in front of us. They scared the wits out of each other and took off in opposite directions. Lady Joe was still slippery, and she greased right out from under me. It took a minute to realize I was on the ground. I jumped up and looked around, but she was, well, gone."

"You mean running?"

"I mean gone, like she wasn't there anymore. It was like I had dreamed about Lady Joe and the mule deer. I was all alone up there, looking at the Pacific Ocean. It took a minute to realize what happened. When it hit me, I started running around and hollering for her like a crazy man."

"Did you round up a few hands to organize a search?"

"I didn't say what we were looking for, but I did saddle up a couple of the boys. We scoured the hills until it got dark. It was like trying to figure out where a bolt of lightning had gone. The next day, we went out again but a light rain settled in, and after that it was hopeless."

"What about notifying the sheriff's department?"

"No way, Jimbo. They left me in charge. Think about that. 'Lee Estes Loses Lady Joe!' It would be all over television and in the newspapers. I'd be running from scandal sheet reporters like some deadbeat celebrity six months behind on child support. Wade Sanchez would catch hell for leaving me in charge, and my old man would come looking for me because I let down Mr. Walker. This thing is beyond catastrophe, Jimbo. It's so bad I can't even think of a word for it."

Jim pondered all of this from under his hat. "You do realize Lady Joe is going to turn up somewhere eventually?"

"The way I see it, if she's not reported missing, either somebody will take her in, or she'll end up in a rescue facility. Nobody is going to suspect in a million years that she's Lady Joe. They'll just figure somebody didn't want her. She's a fine horse, Jimmy. She'll be all right."

"Where did you get Spooks?"

"Well, with a buyer flying in from Dallas I needed to come up with a blue roan mare. I hit the Internet and spent the last couple days driving all up and down the

San Joaquin looking at them. Picked up Spooks for two hundred and fifty dollars. She's pretty much in the ballpark for Lady Joe."

"Except she can't cut."

"We have Mary Jane for that."

"For tomorrow."

"Walker says the man's not a horse person, Jimbo! He doesn't intend to show her at cuttings. He doesn't know a thing about that stuff. He just wants a saddle horse to entertain guests in his backyard. Spooks will suit him fine."

Jim sat forward now, pushing the hat from his face, trying to make sure he was following all this.

"What took me by surprise," Lee continued, "was when this Dallas lawyer calls and says to enter Lady Joe in a little weekend cutting while he's out here. He expects me to ride her so he can get some action pictures for his wall. I think he wants a few of himself standing alongside her in the arena too. Thank God Francine came through with Mary Jane."

"There's something haywire about all this," Jim pondered. "Why would a man pay four hundred thousand dollars for a saddle horse to entertain guests in his back yard?"

"Well, he's from Dallas, so go figure."

"Say again?"

"Those people shoot a different game of pool. I've been there, and it's not Fort Worth or Weatherford."

"Dallas is Weatherford country. Those people know horses."

"Not this jake. Walker says he's some kind of high-profile criminal defense attorney. I don't believe he's ever been on a horse. We could probably sell him a cow and get away with it."

Jim threw his hat on the dashboard and pressed his hands against his face in thought. "Are you sure we can run two different horses past this fellow as Lady Joe?"

"Pretty sure, Jimbo."

"In twenty-four hours? You don't think that's maybe pushing it?"

"Well, it's why I need you with me to meet him."

"What am I supposed to do?"

"You're a good bullshitter, Jimmy. I need you to sell him on Spooks."

"Hey, you're the one who makes up stories! I don't bullshit people."

"That's what I'm talking about. You're a sincere guy. When you say something, people believe it. I need you to tell him it's her and make a big fuss over what a beautiful animal she is."

"No way am I going to say some two-hundred-and-fifty-dollar horse is Lady Joe. I'm sorry, Lee. That's where I draw the line."

Lee knew Jim was like that. "Well, stand next to her, then, while I say it."

Jim shook his head in dismay. "I don't know if I'm ready for this."

Lee took the exit to the airport.

"All we need to do is throw this chicken into the air, Jimbo," Lee assured him. "She's going to fly like a bird."

CHAPTER 5
ROTTEN SCOTT

N ed Pederson dropped into Santa Barbara on a commuter shuttle that had skipped up the coast out of LAX.

There wasn't much cowboy about the short, ruddy-faced attorney, but his dark, conservative suit and debonair necktie suggested a man who could mix up a hostile witness or shake a generous judgment out of a jury. It was a gift that allowed him to support a somewhat naggy wife and two teenaged daughters on a spacious estate outside Dallas. There they lived comfortably alongside two tennis courts and a swimming pool with submerged bar stools that allowed guests to enjoy poolside drinks while in the pool, and they awoke each morning to the pleasant gurgle of an artificial waterfall that replenished the pool. There was ample acreage in the back for horses, though this possibility had not occurred to him until a young intern at Pederson & Wills brought a mare named Lady Joe to his attention.

Ned had knocked back a couple on Southwest out of Dallas but was cut off after propositioning a flight attendant. They did not serve alcohol on the commuter, and by the time it put down in Santa Barbara, he was red-faced and sweaty.

Ned's wife kept him on a short leash over in the Big D, but it crossed his mind that he and Lee Estes might make the acquaintance of some exciting women while talking horses in a California bar. He quickly scanned the terminal for watering holes and spotted a couple of prospects.

"Hey, cowboy," he said when Lee connected by phone. "Where the hell are you, bud?"

"They won't let us past security without a ticket," Lee told him. "You need to meet us in baggage. Look for a couple of dudes in cowboy hats."

Ned took the escalator and watched glumly as a wall of liquor bottles in an overpriced bar quietly disappeared from sight. Lee was waiting with some other fellow near the baggage carousel.

"Welcome to California, Mr. Pederson," Lee said with a confident handshake. "Come point out your luggage for me."

"Well, a man of action! I like that, Lee." Ned pointed to his things, and Lee deftly plucked them from the carousel and swung them over to Jim, who set them aside.

"How was your flight?"

"Good enough." Ned wanted a goddamn drink and was looking for an opportunity to suggest hunting up a little fun before heading out to the ranch. But Lee seemed to have a lot on his mind and was annoyingly focused on matters at hand.

"Mr. Pederson, this is my partner and lifelong friend, Jim Harrison."

"Pleasure, sir," Jim said respectfully, offering his hand.

Ned had not been told of Jim, but the young man looked affable enough and revived his hopes. Ned's experience was that two men in a bar is a private conversation, while three is more casual and likely to attract fun girls.

"Jim, let me tell you a story," Ned blurted out. He leaned closer, as if sharing confidential information. "A fellow was home one night watching television when the sheriff knocks on his door. Sheriff says, 'I hate to bother you, sir, but need to know if your wife is home.' The fellow says, 'No, she's out and about somewhere.' The sheriff looks worried when he hears that and asks, 'Well, do you have a picture of her I can see?' Fellow brings him one. Sheriff looks at the picture. His face drops, and he shakes his head and says, 'Sir, I hate to tell you this, but it looks like your wife's been hit by a truck.' The fellow says to the sheriff, 'I know it, but she cooks good, and she's a wildcat in bed.'"

Pederson laughed so hard that people walking past glanced over at them. The boys just stood there. Lee was too rattled about whether he could run Spooks past Ned as Lady Joe to understand the story. Jim was unable to follow it because his mind was scattered about what Francine was going to say to him that night. Ned had hoped to warm them to the prospect of hunting up some exciting women with a funny story, but the joke had fallen flat.

They crossed the parking lot to the truck, where Jim loaded his things in the back. Ned took a final shot. "Say, where's a good watering hole around here? I need to buy you fellows a drink."

"No problem there. I have a whole liquor cabinet laid out for you at the house," Lee said, helping with the last of his things. Lee was in a hurry to get to the ranch to see what Ned would make of Spooks. Nonetheless, as they were about to squeeze into the cab, it occurred to him to offer a courtesy to his guest. "Say, we do have a minute if you want to call your wife to let her know you arrived safely."

"Oh, hell. Let's get out of here," Ned told him.

It was a little over an hour's drive from Goleta to the Walker Ranch in the Ojai Valley, but Lee called ahead for the house staff to have a whiskey sour prepared for their buyer.

Mr. Walker had apparently alerted the staff that somebody important was on the way. When they pulled up at the main residence, the house manager, Victor Gutierrez, awaited with Pederson's whiskey sour. "Mr. Walker says we are to make you a happy man during your stay in California," Victor cheerfully assured him.

"Oh my, this is good," Pederson said when he sipped the whiskey. "Line up a few more of these, and you won't hear a peep out of me." He chuckled.

Two servants retrieved his luggage from the bed of the truck.

"Victor, I need to show Mr. Pederson a horse," Lee told the house manager. "We'll be back in a few minutes, and then he's all yours."

Lee swung the pickup over to a round pen where Spooks was waiting patiently to impress them. The mare had apparently never seen the inside of a round pen before and looked mixed-up about what to make of such surroundings; she stood quietly toward the center, where nothing about it could jump out at her.

"Oh my Lord, would you look at that?" Ned whispered in awe when he caught sight of her. He was squeezed between Jim and Lee in the cab and was straining to see. "There she is! Lady Joe! It's her all right, and my sweet Jesus if she's not the prettiest blue roan mare to ever walk God's earth."

They slid from the truck, but Lee motioned for Jim and Ned to wait there a minute. He opened the gate, walked up to Spooks, and stroked her neck to get her settled. Once she was reassured, he nodded for Jim and Ned to approach.

"Oh, merciful Lord in heaven, this is one magnificent animal!" Ned spoke again in awe. "Can I touch her?"

"Hold out your hand and let her get your scent," Jim suggested. Ned did this, and to his delight, Spooks lazily displayed the curiosity to sniff it and thereby acknowledge his presence.

"Go ahead and stroke her now," Jim said.

Ned touched her, cautiously at first, and then began stroking her neck when he saw she would tolerate it. She appeared somewhat indifferent.

"Don't look like she's got a whole lot of pep, though," Ned said.

"If a cow was around, her ears would pop right up," Lee assured him. "She's sort of resting right now."

Ned seemed to accept that. He stepped back to look her up and down, nodding with approval.

"Boys, there's a story about this horse nobody in the world knows but me and a young intern in my office. I'm going to tell it to you now."

Jim and Lee exchanged a look. They could not imagine a Lady Joe story they had not heard.

"I'm not a horse person. I'm a criminal defense attorney," Pederson began. "If you boys should ever get in trouble with the law in Dallas, Pederson & Wills is who you want to see. We don't come cheap, but you won't see any jail time. We're the best there is because we've worked the longest and hardest at it. You can't buy experience with money. One thing I know about life is that when push comes to shove, it's not what you've done but how you talk about it in court."

"Mr. Walker speaks very highly of you," Lee said. "I don't know much about that stuff, but he says you're the best."

"Either of you boys ever hear of Cravilli, Stank & Morrow?"

"I don't even know what that is," Lee said.

"They're fairly recent. Well, they've been around and everybody knows who they are, but they only recently put together a firm. Anyway, they've been beating us to a few clients. It's aggravating because not one of them can hold a candle to our experience. It's starting to affect our bottom line, so there you are."

Lee and Jim did not in fact know where they were, but overall, things did not appear to be going badly, so neither of them said anything.

"Look here," Ned continued, "let me ask you something else. Either of you boys heard of Rotten Scott?"

That name got their attention. "Tippy Morrow's bay gelding," Jim said slowly after a pause. "I hear he chases cows for fun, even when nobody's looking. Say, is Tippy the same Morrow as in—?"

Pederson nodded. "That bitch has been stealing our clients with a goddamn horse. Can you believe it? Jim, if you were in deep trouble with the law, would you hire some attorney because he owns a horse? What in the hell is that? But I'm one son of a goddamn bitch if it's not the truth!" Ned looked into his empty whiskey glass. "Say, I could use another of these."

Lee popped open his phone and told Victor to have somebody use the golf cart to run out a whiskey sour.

Ned carried on. "Every time Rotten Scott wins another championship, they celebrate with ad space and TV spots like it was the second coming of Jesus Christ. 'Cravilli, Stank & Morrow! Proud owners of Rotten Scott!' And there's Tippi with that damn gelding, though you can hardly see her behind the mountains of buckles and plaques and lists of championships and lifetime earnings and I don't know what else. I swear to God you're going to think I'm shittin' you, but this is the truth—they tried to run a silhouette of a fiery red mustang stallion for a company logo. The Ford Motor Company rattled their cage and they backed off, but can you imagine? Each week they have a catchy new slogan: *When the Stakes Are High, You Want the Very Best on Your Team.* Or *We Back Winners.* What is the matter with people that when their lives are on the line, they will go out and hire a defense firm because it owns a goddamn horse?"

A whispering golf cart swept up from the main residence with a whiskey sour. The driver handed it to Jim through the fence boards. Ned took a sip and calmed down. He stepped back a little and ran his eyes over Spooks again while sipping the drink.

"Now let me tell you about Lady Joe," he said. "We have a young genius out of law school over in the office. He did some number crunching and came up with this. Nobody believed it at first, but we vetted the bastard, and I swear to God it's true. Lady Joe is, scientifically speaking, what experts call a mathematical anomaly."

Jim and Lee were lost again.

"She's no Rotten Scott," Ned clarified. "You can talk career points, lifetime earnings, championships won and, hey, there's no contest. Point taken. But you can't escape the anomaly. There's maybe a dozen or so times these two horses competed in the same class at the same event. Every time that happened—hear me now—Lady Joe edged out Rotten Scott on points. I'm talking every time. Think about that."

The boys did. "You know it for sure?" Lee frowned.

"It is a proven mathematical certainty. Our young genius discovered this, and we've had several people confirm it. Okay, in the big picture, it don't mean squat, and I will grant you that. Lifetime earnings, career points, championships—squat. But you can't get past mathematical fact. Whenever they competed in the same event, Lady edged him out. Head to head, she whupped him every time. Simple truth."

Jim had to push back his hat a little to scratch his head. "I'll take your word on it, but I have to admit that is an unusual statistic."

"Jim, the minute my people confirmed this, I tracked down Walker and told him to just name his price. I said to pick a number, because I want this horse, and I'll tell you why. The louder they brag about Rotten Scott, the more people I'm going to invite over to my house for dinner and a pony ride on the mare that whupped him. If their motto is *We Back Winners*, ours is *We Whupped Rotten Scott*." Ned chuckled. "That ought to chap Tippy Morrow's ass. Say, maybe I'll send her a can of Monkey Butt, compliments of Pederson & Wills."

The boys pondered all of this but were not sure they had followed everything correctly.

"Do you want to buy the horse?" Lee asked tentatively.

"Hell yes, I want the goddamn horse!" Ned said. "But I want pictures too. I want to see her shut down some cows tomorrow. And pictures of me with this lady in the arena. I intend to cover a whole wall in my den to impress dinner guests, and when they finish looking, I'm going to take them outside for a pony ride on this Rotten Scott beater. How about it? Can you boys do that for me?"

"If we draw some good cows, you'll see plenty of action," Lee said.

"I understand Walker hasn't shown her in a while. I have to say she doesn't look particularly interested in much right now."

"Oh, you'll see a whole different animal tomorrow," Lee assured him. "She just needs a whiff of cow."

"What's that?" Ned asked.

"Something like catnip to a cat," Jim added. He was beginning to see potential here for the first time.

"I entered her in a little weekend cutting up in Paso," Lee said. "It's not much, but with fresh cows, this lady will catch fire for sure."

"That's what I want to hear."

"I forgot to mention one thing," Lee added. "Walker doesn't like a lot of people knowing his personal business. Lady Joe would attract a lot of attention, so to keep the sale quiet, we entered her as Spooks."

"You want to ride her as Spooks?" Ned looked startled.

"If it's okay with you."

Ned thought a moment. "I don't give a rat's ass."

"Then we're good."

"I contracted this fellow Josephson out of Bakersfield to haul her to Dallas for me," Ned said. "I'll have him rendezvous with us in Paso Robles. Walker gave me the wire address to transfer payment. Lee, he says you have access to the papers on this horse?"

"I'll surrender them the minute Walker confirms the transfer," Lee told him.

"Well then, boys," Ned said, "Let's make this happen."

"That's wonderful. We'll sure do that, Mr. Pederson." Lee looked hugely relieved. "Let me drop you off at the house so Victor can refresh that drink. Then I need to run Jim back home. He'll rendezvous with us in Paso mañana."

"Mañana," Pederson agreed.

CHAPTER 6

LEE'S NERVOUS BREAKDOWN

Lee pulled out from the ranch, across a cattle guard, and onto a county blacktop that ran past abundant pastureland and through Ojai to the interstate. As they cranked up to speed, Jim slid down in the shotgun seat and again pulled his hat low over his eyes to escape into the safety of darkness.

"So how would you say this thing is going?" he asked from somewhere under the hat.

"I'd say it's a done deal."

"Explain that to me."

"Well, you heard the man. He loves Spooks."

There was a moment of silence. Jim spoke frankly from under his hat. "Lee, I'm scared to death this thing is going to blow up and go all haywire on us somehow."

"Never happen, compadre."

"You sure?"

"Say, we have a solid lead on this mallard. All we need to do now is take the shot."

They drove a little in silence.

"How many laws you figure we broke?" Jim asked.

"I fail to see where anybody is getting hurt here, Jimbo."

"We're selling a saddle horse for middle six figures. There's got to be a felony in there somewhere."

"The way I see it, we're just making people happy. Pederson wants a blue roan mare and Lady Joe's papers. Well, we're fixing him up with that. Walker, meanwhile, sees a chance to take four hundred big ones off this jake for Lady Joe. We're going to close that deal for him. Jimmy, we're the good guys here."

Jim allowed that to pass. "So how is this going to work, exactly?"

"Well, me and Pederson bring Spooks up to Paso in the morning. You want to get there early. Park Mary Jane as far from the arena as you can. Then walk over to the entrance and meet us. I'll leave Pederson with you; show him around the facility and find some good spots where he can take pictures. While you're doing that, I'll go find your truck and park alongside it. Spooks will stay in the trailer. I'll unload Mary Jane and bring her to the warm-up pen."

Jim pondered this from under his hat and could not think of anything wrong with it. "I guess that should work," he said finally.

"You sit on the back fence and pick out some good cows for me. Let's show that lawyer how to shut down a heifer. We'll give him some pictures that jump off the wall at his guests. We can do this, Jimbo. We've picked a lot of good cows for each other, and we both had some good runs back in the day."

"Francine's been so busy with a career, she hasn't shown Mary Jane in a while."

"If that horse has any cow left in her, I'll find it."

"So what kind of numbers are we looking for?"

"Well, I'd like to put a seventy-two on the board. Don't guess it matters a whole lot if Pederson gets his action shots. Probably it would impress him if we could make it into the second Go Round, though."

"Mary Jane ought to be able to do that."

"Then we're good."

Jim fell back into silence under his hat. Horses grazed peacefully behind the white board fences along the passing countryside.

"What about the next part?" Jim asked. "How do we switch back for the trade?"

"You stay with Pederson. After my final run, I'll tie Mary Jane to your trailer and then bring Spooks around front. Walker is going to call from Switzerland to confirm the transfer of funds. Then I surrender Lady Joe's papers to Pederson. The Bakersfield fellow will be there to haul Spooks off to Dallas for him."

"And that's it?"

"We're done. I'll help you load Mary Jane, and you can take her home to your wife."

Jim sat up and pushed the hat back from his face. Everything looked to be going as slick as a highway after a rain, but he was still in a blue funk.

"God, I sure hope she doesn't quit me, Lee."

"She won't. Not after this."

"She might. Maybe even tonight. She's been talking about going back to law school."

"Jimbo, think about it. Walker's off in Switzerland and this huge deal drops out of the sky, and guess what? It's us—we nailed it for him."

"You think it's impressive enough for him to pull us into the horse business?"

"Well, we're looking at four hundred thousand for Lady Joe. I'd say that's impressive."

"He doesn't know you lost Lady Joe."

"We got that covered, Jimbo."

"Still, it's sort of a big one."

"Nobody's going to know. It's all good."

"I guess what I need to hear you say is there's no way this thing can go all haywire. I'm really scared of losing my wife, Lee."

"We're going to close this deal, and Francine's not going to leave you. Are we good now?"

Jim considered a moment and yielded to Lee's confidence. "Okay, I'm good."

Lee nodded in satisfaction. "Nothing's going haywire," he added.

They drove a little further in silence, and it looked like the matter was settled. Lee was pleased with himself for having persuaded Jim of the soundness of the scheme, and rolled that accomplishment around in his head with satisfaction. Then it occurred to him that what he had said to Jim was pure hustle. Lee had blundered into so much trouble in his short life that he had acquired the art of fast talk as a survival skill. But no amount of fast talk would save him if this thing went haywire and his old man found out.

"Oh, boy!" Lee whispered in a sudden panic.

Jim looked over at him.

Lee had a funny look on his face, and his hands began to shake on the steering wheel. Then he started talking to himself. "Oh, boy, oh, boy, oh, boy!" he muttered excitedly.

"Hey, are you okay?"

"I need to pull over, Jimbo. Oh, boy, oh, boy!"

Lee swung off the blacktop to stop in a dry grassy ditch. He threw the door open, slid out, and tried to walk quickly away, but then his legs went all wobbly on him. Somehow, he managed to sit down and lie flat on his back in the grass, looking up at blue sky.

Jim slid out the other side and went to check on him.

"Lee, what exactly do you think you're doing, if you don't mind my asking?"

"Shoot me, Jimmy. I'm dying down here."

"Say that again?"

"There's no way in hell this is going to work. I don't know what I was thinking. Aw, Jimmy! It's going to go straight down a rat hole!"

"You just said we were good."

"I'm full of shit! Don't you know that by now? We're going to mess this up good. Oh, man! Papa's going to find out about it too."

"How would he find out?"

"All he has to do is look at me. He'll say, 'Lee, did you lose Lady Joe?' And I'll say, 'Yes, sir. I sure did. I lost her ass good!'"

"Why in the world would he even ask that?"

"Because he knows stuff, Jimbo! He knows! He can tell by looking at me."

"Nobody knows but us."

"He's going to find out I let down Mr. Walker and come straight after my sorry ass, Jimmy."

"He's not going to find out! Anyway, how are you letting Walker down? This deal is huge, and we're brokering it for him. We're going to be in the horse business."

"What if Pop asks me, Jimmy? What if he does? What should I say?"

"He's not going to ask."

"He might."

"Lee, don't start with that. You pulled me into this. I'm in up to my neck too. We can do it—we have to! Don't fall apart on me now. Snap out of it!"

Lee just lay there, looking at the sky.

"Lee, will you get up from the damn ditch?"

"How about we turn the truck around and head for Mexico?"

"No, you want to get out of the ditch and take me home to my wife."

There was a moment of silence.

"Tell me it's going to work, and maybe I'll get up," Lee said.

"It's going to be fine."

"What makes you think so?"

"Well, it's the only thing I've got going that might impress my wife enough to stay. Anyway, we both know horses. We can do this."

"What if Pops finds out I lost Lady Joe?"

"He won't. Lady Joe's probably found a real nice home somewhere. The only thing your pop will know is what a wonderful thing you did for Mr. Walker. He's going to be real proud of you."

"You wouldn't shit me, Jimmy?"

"Well, I was skeptical at first, but swear to God I think this might actually work. It's a chance to show folks what we can do. We might actually amount to something for once. And Francine won't quit me."

"Let me rest for a minute and think about it."

"Okay, partner, you do that. Remember, I'm shaking in my boots, too." Jim sighed and went back in the cab to sit and wait for him.

Eventually Lee got to his feet, went quietly back to the truck, and started the engine. They sat listening to the engine for a minute or so.

Finally, Lee put the truck in gear and drove his friend home.

CHAPTER 7
MARRIAGE TROUBLE

Francine would turn twenty-four in the fall and was thinking about leaving her husband. She was driving to work at the law office where they had to prepare for a court hearing on Monday. Her mind was swimming with conflicted emotions over what had just happened at home. Jim was hanging out with Lee again, and this only confirmed to her how far apart she and her husband had drifted.

Since she had gone to work as a paralegal at Evans, Sangster & Longtree, a whole new world was opening up to her. She spent her days among educated professionals who casually engaged in small talk about Middle Eastern politics or the merits of current Federal Reserve fiscal policy. They were attorneys who litigated seven- and eight-figure lawsuits during the week and went sailing or played tennis on weekends. And they accomplished these things as casually as Jim and Lee might while away an afternoon shooting pool in a bar.

Francine had been invited on several occasions to attend company socials at the country club with her husband, but she was afraid Jim would be lost there and have no idea what to say to such people. She had also begun thinking about going to law school and passing the bar; that prospect excited her, but she realized it would only further shut Jim out of her world.

She knew that if she were going to leave him, she should do it now, before they had children. She wanted a family but did not want her children to grow up in an emotionally confusing cycle of visitations between separated parents. About such things, a girl had to be practical.

And yet she hesitated. She felt safe married to Jim because he made her feel needed and secure. Jim was crazy about her and would never lie or cheat on her, and she knew he would always come home at night. He was a loyal and loving husband and, she had to admit, had the potential to be a good father. It scared her a little to realize that if she left him, she might never again find someone so devoted to her.

Francine knew men found her attractive because they hit on her a lot in bars, restaurants, and airports. She once had a strange experience when a man she did not know followed her for several blocks down the street, excitedly declaring she was the most thrilling woman he had ever seen in his life, and he wanted her to be the mother of his children. She finally escaped into a drug store to get rid of him. Another time, the office air-conditioning was being serviced, and she overheard a repairman say to his assistant, "I'd wreck that like a *Jackass* Porsche."

But Francine did not believe there was anything particularly interesting or special about her. She was scared most men would realize this after living with her a little while and would lose interest and leave her for someone more exciting. Jim would never do that, but she knew it happened to a lot of girls. Francine believed thrilling women existed and were out there but did not think she was one of them.

By eight o'clock that night, Francine was still at work in the conference room, and it was clear they were not anywhere near ready for court on Monday. Everyone had left except Robert Sangster and her, and he had wilted about an hour ago. His jacket had slipped from a chair to the floor, and he was sprawled facedown, asleep on a couch. At thirty-four, Bob was the youngest of the partners but was already living with a wife and three children in a beautiful split-level in the foothills above the city. Though ambitious and to all appearances living the good life, at the moment even he was dead to the world.

Francine pushed doggedly ahead, working by herself at the littered conference table, scrolling through case files for precedent on her laptop.

The firm represented plaintiff Loretta Morgan, who had been expelled from a national cutting horse association for riding Non-Pro in cutting competitions. Someone informed the association by anonymous letter that she was a professional barrel racer who taught that discipline on a horse ranch she owned with her husband. As a professional, of course, she wasn't permitted to ride in Non-Pro events.

Sangster met with the association to argue that barrel racing was a rodeo sport unrelated to cutting and should have no effect on her Non-Pro cutting status. The association felt that as a private organization, they could draw up and interpret their own rules as they saw fit, and acceptance of that authority was a condition of membership.

Evans, Sangster & Longtree filed suit at the state level to complain that the association's misinterpretation of an ambiguously worded rule caused significant decline in the monetary value of Ms. Morgan's cutting horses due to her inability to show them. The association's attorneys moved to dismiss the complaint, because only the association has authority to interpret association rules—and on this point of law, the outcome of a $5.2-million lawsuit now rested.

On Monday, a judge would hear opposing arguments about whether the State of California could interpret the rules of a private organization. The court decision would set a precedent with far-reaching consequences, but immediately at stake was the reputation of Ms. Morgan and the financial worth of fourteen cutting horses.

Francine was by now familiar with much of equine-related law but was less acquainted with the scope of state authority over such matters. Somewhere in the ocean of case law on her laptop, she believed, must be the precedent that would save Ms. Morgan's cutting horses from obscurity.

Bob Sangster woke from his nap and rolled onto his back on the couch. He was still groggy from sleep and lay watching Francine work in silence; he was impressed with her intense concentration and then fascinated by the bright red dress and jet-black hairband across her blond hair.

"That dress is scorching hot," he observed. "Where did you find it?"

"It was on sale." She laughed. "But thank you."

"Stay away from the chaparral in that. We're in fire season, you know. You'd ignite the stuff, and the whole county would be toast."

"You can go back to sleep now, Bob."

He stretched his arms and chuckled. "Oh, Francine, Francine. Why couldn't I have met a girl like you before I married?"

"A girl like what?"

"You understand how hard it is to make money. My wife thinks we just shake it out of trees. Sure, we knock down some big paydays, but you're here every day and see what we have to go through. Aggie has no idea. She spends it like water."

"A lot of people would like to have your life."

"Francine, sometimes I get home from work wiped out, and Aggie's falling to pieces because some store clerk made a remark that upset her. I'm supposed to listen to that and sympathize after a full day in the office. She says I don't care about my family. I get no appreciation from her for what we do here at all."

"It sounds like you two need to talk some things out."

"I suppose, but I'm getting tired of it." He retrieved his jacket from the floor. "Anyway, we should call it a night. You ready?"

"Give me a minute." She was still scrolling through the precedents.

"What's Jim up to these days? Still at the restaurant?"

"He was just promoted to assistant manager."

"You know what I think? I think we married the wrong people. You should go back to law school, and after you pass the bar, we should both get divorced. Then we can move to Los Angeles and go into entertainment law. I'm tired of these bullshit billionaires suing each other over horses. Let's manage movie stars and attend Oscar parties together."

"Now I know you've been working too hard," she said, stopping to read a precedent.

Bob came up behind her as she worked and began quietly massaging her shoulders. It surprised her for a moment, but then it felt good, so she relaxed a little and allowed it.

"I think this girl has earned a drink," he said.

She often had drinks with the partners after work, but this was the first time anyone had asked her to go alone.

"Okay, we're done here," she replied abruptly, closing the laptop. "Let's go home."

She gathered up her things, but when she went to the door, Bob stood there, blocking it.

"What are we doing?" she asked.

He placed a finger near her breast and ran it lightly down the length of her body. "I want to take off this dress," he said.

She could not believe that Robert Sangster was hitting on her. Francine discovered, to her surprise, that she was not sure what she wanted to do about it.

"Why don't I take you to dinner tonight? They have a good menu at the Country Inn. Then we can pick out a good bottle of wine and check into a room for a while. I'll have you back here by midnight, two o'clock tops."

She did not say anything.

"Francine?"

"Mr. Sangster, I think you need to go home to your wife," she said finally.

He acceded gracefully. "Hey, I gave it a shot. No harm, no foul, right?"

"Sure."

"Are we all right?"

"I'll see you in the morning, Mr. Sangster."

He opened the door, and she slipped out ahead of him and was gone.

It was almost nine when she got home, and Jim was sitting on the couch waiting for her. He was scared to death about what she was going to say—about him bringing Lee home, them riding Mary Jane tomorrow, and the money for fresh cows. It was a lot to talk about.

Francine closed the front door behind her and walked past him into the kitchen without a word. She got a glass of orange juice from the refrigerator, and it seemed to Jim that she was more upset about something than angry.

"How did it go?" he asked hopefully.

"We still have a lot to do."

She came from the kitchen and past him again to the bathroom, where she took a couple of aspirin with the orange juice. Then she removed the headband, shook out her hair, and slipped out of the dress.

She looked in on Jim, who was still waiting on the couch.

"Jim, I have a headache, and we still have a lot to do tomorrow. Do you mind sleeping in the other bedroom tonight?"

"Oh, sure!" he agreed, relieved that nothing bad was going to happen, at least for now.

Jim lay awake in the other bedroom until after midnight. It occurred to him they had not exchanged a goodnight kiss, which was a longstanding rule, whether they were on speaking terms or not.

He crept into their bedroom, where she was asleep, her long hair partially covering her face as it fell across the edge of the bed. He knelt beside her and, carefully pushing back the hair, gave her a gentle peck on the cheek.

"Oh!" She jumped awake, startled. "Jim? What's happening?" She was groggy and confused.

"Shhh!" he murmured. "It's okay. I'm sorry, sugar."

"What are you doing?"

"I just remembered that you didn't get your goodnight kiss. I didn't mean to wake you."

"Oh, okay," she said.

"I'm sorry if I scared you."

"You didn't scare me."

"I woke you, though."

"No, it's okay. That was sweet of you. You shouldn't have bothered, though. I was so mean to you today."

"Well, we sure gave you a lot to be upset about. Listen, I want you to know me and Lee are really going to try to do good tomorrow. It looks like an opportunity to maybe impress some important money people, and Lee has to show Mr. Walker he can run the ranch without messing up. Horses is about the only thing we're any good at, but it takes money. Somebody might back us to the point we could amount to something. I know it's not much, but I just don't see a whole lot else out there for us."

"Well, just go try your heart out, then. That's all anybody can do. I'm sorry I was so mean today."

"I'm crazy about you, Francine," he said, touching her hair again. "I think about you every minute of every day."

"You shouldn't. There's nothing special about me, Jim."

"There's a lot special about you to me."

"Jim, you need to get that out of your head. I'm just me, and there's a dozen other girls just like me on every corner who would be lucky to have you. They would treat you better, too."

"Hey, I'll see you tomorrow," he whispered. He started to go.

"Jim, come back here," she said.

When he turned back, she sat up, threw her arms around him, and embraced him tightly, and then she kissed him on his cheeks, forehead, nose, and finally gave him a peck on the mouth. "Okay, now get out of here," she said.

Jim went back to the other bedroom.

The next morning, he was up at dawn getting Mary Jane ready to load into the trailer. He fixed some coffee, made a cup for Francine, and set it on her nightstand. Then he pulled out with Mary Jane for Paso. Francine did not wake up until nine and got to work a little after ten.

CHAPTER 8
SALLY TEMPLE

L ee awoke before dawn feeling like he had been holding his breath the whole night. He lay in bed, trying to think about what he and Jim had missed that was going to trip them up. For the life of him, he could not put a finger on anything. Daybreak reassured him that there was still furniture in his room, and the world had not disappeared on him in the darkness of night. If he could only keep focused and do the next thing in front of him, and if his legs did not go all wobbly on him again, it was going to be all right.

He felt more confident after loading Spooks into the trailer. He walked over to the big house to find Pederson in high spirits over the fine breakfast Victor had prepared.

"Morning, Lee!" Ned called cheerfully. "Say, I'm so excited, I've been thinking horses all night. I might be picking up things. Take what you said yesterday about how Lady Joe will pop her ears back when she sees a cow? I think I see what's going on. I bet she has some snake in her."

"How do you figure?"

"Well, she's so amiable, a fellow might not think she was much of a champion. That's like a snake. They look harmless enough until you step on one. When you put a cow in front of Lady Joe, it's like stepping on a snake."

"She might have some snake in her." Lee nodded agreeably.

He was content to let Ned linger over breakfast. Lee wanted a late start so Jim would have plenty of time to get to Paso Robles with Mary Jane. Jim was going to park her somewhere in the back lot and then walk around to the main entrance on foot to meet them. Lee would drop Pederson off with Jim and then swing Spooks around back next to Mary Jane. He had run the plan through his mind so many times that he was convinced it did not have a flaw.

Pederson finished breakfast and was eager to move. They took the county road to Ojai and then picked up the interstate though San Luis Obispo and the Cuesta Pass into the south end of the Salinas Valley. The transverse mountains, San Andreas, and coastal mountains of this area form a great triangle. Pederson gazed in amazement. He was from the Texas lowlands around Dallas and had never seen such country.

"We're in luck," Lee told him. "You're going to take your pictures at the event center, where they have a real nice enclosed arena. Calicut is just a small local cutting club, the only thing I could find on such short notice. They usually hold cuttings at somebody's ranch. I guess nothing's up in Paso this weekend, so Calicut gets to use the facility."

Ned could not have looked more pleased about how the day was going.

They came up the 101 into Paso Robles, and Lee pulled off the highway into the event center. Though it was only a small local cutting, other trailers were arriving with horses, and a bustle of men, women, and children drifted across the lot toward the arena.

Jim was nowhere in sight. Lee pulled clear of the entrance and stopped alongside the Calicut trailer office. They sat for a few minutes in silence. "I'm sure he's around somewhere," Lee said. "Help me keep an eye out for him."

"Oh, mercy!" Ned blurted. "Lee, look what I see coming. Please tell me you know this girl."

She was a winsome sun-bronzed cowgirl of nineteen or so with straw-blond hair pulled back in a ponytail, walking toward them with quick, purposeful strides from the enclosed arena.

"Oh, man," Lee groaned, pulling down his hat to hide his face. "It's Sally Temple. Is she headed this way?"

"Like a shot."

Sally was a waitress at the restaurant where Jim worked as assistant manager. She quickly reached them and was in Lee's face at his window.

"Lee Estes, you're a fucking asshole, you know it?"

"Hey, girl, what's up?"

"You don't take somebody home and then disappear in the middle of the night and not call for two months."

"Sally, can we please not talk about personal shit right now? I have a buyer in the truck."

"Who does that? Seriously, who does that? I want to know what girl out of her right mind ever led you to believe you can get away with that."

"This fellow just flew in from Dallas to see a horse."

"Well boohoo and fuck him too! You might just as well turn this rig around and go home. You can't ride today because I told on you."

"Told what?"

"I told Frank you work on the Walker place."

"Goddamn, you silly bitch! What did you do that for?"

"Because fuck you, that's why!"

"Jesus Christ!" Lee turned to Ned. "Mr. Pederson I apologize for the French, but need to speak with the lady about a personal matter."

Ned waved a hand to show he was not in the least offended. Lee slid from the cab and furiously slammed the door. Then he took Sally firmly by the arm and walked her a short distance away.

"Sally Temple, I sure wish you would grow up and start acting like a mature woman. I'm getting real tired of this girly shit."

"Oh, spare me the horse manure. You wouldn't know a mature woman if she bit you in the ass."

"You're acting like some nine-year-old little tattle-tale. 'Ha, ha, ha, you did this to me, so I told on you!' That tit-for-tat shit. That's what I'm talking about."

"I'm sorry, but what goes around comes around. You can give it but can't take it, can you?"

"What? We shoot a few games of pool and you think you can ruin my life?"

"Lee, I couldn't ruin your life if I tried."

"It's one thing to mess with somebody, but you don't fuck with business!"

Jim walked up just then, and they stopped arguing.

"Hey Sal, what's up?" he asked.

"Not much."

"Riding today?"

"Sure. I'm wearing my lucky panties."

Jim realized something was up between them. "Hey, I'm interrupting. I'll let you two talk."

"No, we're done here," she said. "I was just having a discussion with asshole numero uno."

Few things thrilled Ned like a pissed-off woman, and he slid from the truck for a closer look. "Morning, Jim," he said. "I've been looking for somebody to introduce me to the lady."

"Oh, sure." Jim did the honors. "Sally, this is Ned Pederson out of Dallas. Ned, Sally Temple."

Ned could not think of anything to say to her.

"Ever been out this way before?" she asked congenially.

"Not hardly, but I like it. Real nice country you've got here. Real nice."

Lee was agitated and was ignoring everybody, walking in a tight circle, staring at the ground in intense thought.

"You okay over there, partner?" Jim asked.

"Everybody wait here," he snapped. "I need to speak to Frank." He sprang up the Calicut trailer steps and disappeared inside.

Frank Hobart, a weathered horseman and businessman in his mid-forties, looked upset about something too. The minute Lee sprang through the door, Frank cut him off with a wave of his finger.

"Lee, do not open your mouth. I have something to say here and do not want one word out of you until I finish talking." He pointed to a window overlooking the parking lot. "That window is wide open and man did I catch an earful. I almost turned blue in the face. Calicut is just a local little startup, and we're still getting organized. Our mission is to create a wholesome family environment where folks can bring their horses for a little weekend cutting. We've got women and children here. The last thing we need is Lee Estes in a parking-lot squabble with his pool-hall slut. You two need to take that stuff across the highway somewhere and work it out."

"I'm sorry about that, Frank. You see what I'm up against. Anyway, Sally says you cut me from the draw."

"Do you work on the Walker place?"

"I do a little longing but mostly mucking out stalls and washing horses and stuff."

"Do you work cows with their horses?"

"Not enough to call it that."

"You live on the property?"

"Board comes with the job."

"You can't live and work on a cutting horse ranch and ride Non-Pro. You know that."

"Frank, I have a buyer out of Dallas who wants to see a horse work a cow. Walker's in Switzerland, and I promised to take care of it."

"If it was up to me, I could maybe let this slide for Walker's sake," Frank told him. "But we have a charter and rules and a board of directors, and I've just been elected president. We're seeking official PCCHA recognition. If somebody found out about this and complained, it could set us back several years."

"So that's it? Sally Temple can just walk in here and fuck me, just like that? You're going to let her get away with that?"

Frank almost felt sorry for Lee, and despite himself he shook his head and chuckled. "Lee, I have no idea in the world what that was all about out there, but maybe you need to be a little nicer to the ladies. You might have better luck in life."

"This is bullshit!" Lee stormed back to the door and threw it open. Jim was outside with Sally and Ned. "Jim, can you come in here a minute?"

Jim disappeared inside, leaving Ned alone with Sally.

Ned's mind was still racing for something to break the ice with her. "I'll bet you're a wildcat in bed," he ventured.

"You'll never find out," she shot back without missing a beat.

Lee brought Jim over to the desk. "Frank, do you remember Jim Harrison?"

"I believe we've met. Doing all right?"

"Pretty well."

"Listen, Jim," Lee said, "Sally messed up some stuff. It looks like you need to ride in my place."

"I can do that. Sure."

"Hold on." Frank interrupted them. "Lee, nobody's riding in your place. You're scratched."

"Fine. Then Jim will enter."

"He'll have to pay a late fee."

"We'll pay a late fee. Anything else?"

"Who owns the horse?"

"I do."

"He can't ride her. You know the rules."

Jim started to open his mouth. Actually, this was not a problem because he would be riding Mary Jane, a horse owned by his wife and boarded on rental property they cohabited in San Luis Obispo. But he realized it was probably best not to complicate matters with this information, so he did not say anything.

"I'll be right back." Lee was fuming. He stormed out of the trailer, past Sally and Ned, to the truck. "You sure fucked me good this time," he told her as he blew past. He retrieved Spooks's papers from the glove compartment and returned to the office.

"See this?" he said, waving the papers at Frank. He put them on the desk and began writing on them.

"What's happening?" Jim asked.

"Jimbo, you just bought yourself a horse."

"Say again?"

"For one dollar. You can pay me later."

He showed the papers to Jim and then slid them across the desk to Frank. "How about now? Are we good?"

Frank studied them and nodded. Then he removed some forms from a drawer. "Jim, you need to fill out an entry form, and this other form is for the late entry."

Jim took the papers and went to work on them.

"And then I'll need to see a check," Frank added.

"No, you won't," Lee said. "I already paid."

"You're scratched. Your fees are forfeit."

"Jesus Christ! How many ways are you going to fuck us?"

"Okay, let's see." Frank did some calculations. "That's two hundred and fifty for the entry and a one-fifty late fee."

"What about the goddamn cows? I paid five hundred for fresh cows. You gonna fuck me on that too?"

"I suppose Jim can have your cows. I'm not supposed to do that, but I don't guess anybody will notice."

Jim handed over the completed forms. Frank looked them over and found everything in order. "All right, boys. Let me see four hundred dollars, and we're good."

Lee and Jim looked at each other. "I'll be right back," Lee said.

He went back outside to Sally and Ned.

"Mr. Pederson, a situation has come up. I'm real embarrassed to ask this. It's all good—Jim's going to ride—but we need four hundred dollars."

"No problem there," Ned promptly responded. He took a money clip from his pocket and peeled off four crisp hundred-dollar bills. He appeared to think these were normal complications of the horse business.

"I appreciate this," Lee said respectfully. "I'll get back to you pretty quick."

"No, no. I was going to buy you fellas a few drinks anyway."

Lee went back inside and gave the money to Frank. "Let's get out of here," he told Jim.

They went to leave, but Jim paused in the doorway, looking down at Ned and Sally.

"Wait a minute, Lee. How does this work now?"

Lee sighed and shook his head. "Let me think."

Lee went down to Sally. "Come here a minute," he said, pulling her aside by the arm again. "Listen, if you're done fucking with me for today, I need you to do something for me."

"You need what?"

"Dammit, I have to go with Jim. Keep an eye on my buyer for me a few minutes."

"Ha! What am I supposed to do with him?"

"Christ, I don't care. Show him around the arena. Let him find some places to take pictures. Just don't let him get lost."

Before she could reply, he leaped into the cab and drove off with Jim.

They pulled Spooks around back and parked alongside Jim's trailer with Mary Jane. First, they unloaded Spooks and tethered her in a halter to the trailer. Next, they unloaded and tacked up Mary Jane.

Jim mounted her to ride over to the warm-up pen.

"It's pretty much the same game plan, Jimbo. Soon as you're done riding, get Mary Jane back here and tether her. Then walk Spooks around front to me and Pederson. The Bakersfield fellow ought to be there by then to haul her off to Dallas. Are we good?"

"I guess. Lee, I swear to God, whatever this is we're doing, it is not the secret to a long life."

"Compadre, I wish we were off shooting pool somewhere over a couple of cold longnecks."

And he walked off to find his buyer.

CHAPTER 9

BRIGHT EYES

The sport of cutting recalls the days of the open range when horses were used to herd cattle and especially to cut newborn calves from the herd for branding. The first instinct of a separated calf is to get back to the herd and rejoin its mother. A good cutting horse takes a natural delight in preventing "cuts" (the separated calves) from doing that. She will dance and dash, make hard stops and quick reverses, and do pretty much anything else to stay between the calf and herd. The harder a calf tries, the more enthusiastic a good cutting horse becomes about stopping her.

Cutting as a sport takes place in a corral or arena with the calves—always referred to as cows—herded against a side designated the back fence. Only one contestant is allowed in the arena at a time, and the contestant has two and a half minutes to work the herd. The rider's job is to gently take his horse into the herd without scattering it and force a lively young cow out toward the center of the arena. Once a cow has been cut, the rider drops his reins to signal the judges that he is done. Then he grabs the saddle horn and holds tight because now he is mostly along for the ride, and it may be a wild one.

A good cow will try almost anything to get around that horse and back into the herd. The horse must figure out how to shut down every attempt without any visible cues from the rider. If a disheartened cow stops trying and there is time left on the clock, the rider will raise his reins to signal he is quitting that cow and try to cut a livelier one from the herd.

The horse and rider start with seventy points and are awarded or penalized points by judges during the course of a run. Their final score can be as high as eighty or as low as sixty. When all contestants have completed one run, it is called a Go Round. The highest scoring contestants advance to a second Go Round, for which fresh cows are brought in and settled, and then a winner and final rankings for the event are determined.

The major cutting competitions are regional or even national, sponsored by organizations like NCHA or PCCHA and held in enclosed arenas or venues such as the Paso Robles Event Center, South Point in Las Vegas, or the Will Rogers Coliseum in Fort Worth. There, many vendors will set up shop to sell refreshments, boots and tack, horse nutritional supplements, and the latest fashions in equine riding attire.

More modest weekend cuttings by small local clubs are usually hosted on somebody's ranch, though a nearby venue may offer its facilities when available, as the Paso Robles Event Center did for Calicut. Such cuttings draw a smaller, local crowd with few vendors, if any, though you can usually purchase a good ham sandwich and lemonade, and somebody might even bring a guitar for entertainment.

All cuttings are free, and anybody interested enough to show up is welcome. Weekend cuttings tend to resemble small family gatherings rather than a football tailgate party. Most of the people know each other. Nonetheless, unless you are drunk, scaring horses with a bullhorn, or otherwise misbehaving, nobody will ask you to leave. Tell an owner that his or her horse is the most beautiful animal you have ever seen, and you will win an instant friend eager to explain anything you wish to know about horses.

There is something about a sunny day in the country with the smell of horses in the air and the scent of arena dirt, and the company of those who devote their lives to these astonishing animals, that will reassure a pessimist of any political persuasion that, at least for an afternoon, there is still something very right about America. Even the frazzled office worker from the big city who escapes to the country for a local cutting will return to work on Monday with renewed enthusiasm for life.

Jim rode Mary Jane into the warm-up pen where you normally lope a horse to warm her up. Mary Jane knew Jim very well, but they had not worked together in a while, so he wanted to get reacquainted and work out any kinks between them. He began by putting her through a few basics, moving from a walk to a trot to a canter and then to a few turns and even a little spin for fun. She was quite nice on a flying lead change.

Jim was suddenly overwhelmed by a rush of emotion, aware that he was on the animal more precious to Francine than anything else in the world. He felt certain that if he could impress Mary Jane with his horsemanship, she would like him too much to allow Francine to leave him.

Mary Jane had known Jim a long time, but he needed to let her see that he had matured and was a better person now. He took her into a tight turn and was pleased that she looked proud of her execution.

Mary Jane sensed something had changed in him, that Jim was more sure of hand and confident about his intentions. They were working well now on the runs, stops, and turns. Jim could see that she was accepting him and working to please him. Somehow the wires got crossed in his head, and he began to share his thoughts with her.

"Mary Jane, I sure wish you'd put in a good word to Francine for me," he said as he put her through a run. "She's thinking about divorcing me. Please don't let her do that. I don't know what I'd do if she went away. Anyway, I'm afraid something bad might happen to her, because I don't like those lawyer people at all. It's true I don't know anything about them except what I see on television, but it doesn't look like much of a life to me. They shout at each other in court all day about who gets how much money, and that can't be a healthy way to live."

Jim took the mare on a fast run to a hard stop and reversed to take off again in the opposite direction. "I saw one episode where the lawyer got so worked up in court that he needed a drink to calm himself down. After he had a few, he either went out and cheated on his wife or went home and got in an argument and hit her. I forget which, but it was real bad. That's no way for Francine to live. She could end up a bitter, middle-aged alcoholic, meeting with divorce attorneys and attending AA meetings during the day and passing out on the couch all liquored-up at night. I couldn't stand to see a girl like her end up that way."

Now he put the mare through a quick little dance of feint and counterfeint, like you see when a cow is trying to fake her out.

"Mary Jane, I'm going to say something I've never told anyone. The first time I saw Francine, I remember thinking, 'If I can marry this girl, I'll never ask anything of life again.' That's how I felt, but I was too scared to ask her out. Well, she was pretty mad at Lee when she quit him, so she asked if I wanted to take her to the movies. That went well, and she said I could ask her out again if I wanted. And that was how we started dating.

"I don't much look at other girls anymore, because she's the standard I judge them by, and there's no sense trading down from the best. For some reason everything about her is exactly right with me. I like how she turns her wrist when she holds a fork, the words she chooses when she says something, and the rhythm of her voice when she talks. I like the clothes she wears and how she walks a little bit different in each outfit.

"Please tell her these things, Mary Jane, because she would think I was crazy if I said them, and otherwise I don't guess she will ever know. I wish I could give her a million dollars, but I don't see how I will ever come up with that kind of money. I promise you this, though. That girl will never fall in harm's way on my watch. I'll look after her for both of us and make sure she always feels warm and safe.

"Please tell her this, Mary Jane. You don't have to say it all at once. Start out slow. Sometime when she's looking the other way, maybe come up from behind and whisper in her ear. Start with something simple like, 'Don't leave Jim. Don't leave Jim.' If she walks off, don't get discouraged. Go up to her again and whisper some more. If she's sitting under a tree, that might be an opportunity to get more elaborate. You could say, 'Francine, I sure like Jim a lot and hope you don't send him away, because I like having him around.' Something like that. You need to go slow with Francine. Mary Jane, if you'll consider this, I swear to you that I will put one fine cow in front of you in just a few minutes."

He estimated Mary Jane was tuned up about right and walked her over to wait their run. The order of riders is selected by draw, but because of his late entry, he was riding at the bottom of the set.

When Jim rode Mary Jane into the arena for their run, he immediately confronted a serious problem that had completely slipped his mind. Because of the change in riders and everything else going on, neither he nor Lee had had an opportunity to study the cows. Lee was up in the bleachers with Pederson, where they had found a good position to take action shots. Sally was no longer with them because she was riding today. Jim would have to make the best of things the way they were.

His two and a half minutes did not begin until he took Mary Jane across the time line toward the herd, so he sat for a moment, studying the cows. They were well settled, and his added cows were sufficient to assure not all had been worked, but he could not make out much else about them from there.

You did not want one that had been worked because she might be discouraged and not try very hard. But you didn't want one that was too wild either, because there was no telling what it might do; in some venues, it might even try to escape up into the bleachers. Nor did you want a zombie that just stood there looking at you like she was in some kind of fog. And you certainly did not want one with an infected eye; she would not be able to see very well and might run into you. The trick was to pick a healthy and intelligent-looking cow that, once cut, would try in the worst way to get back into the herd. That would give Mary Jane opportunity to show her stuff and run up some points. But you had to study the cows ahead of time, and it was too late for that.

One of the turnback riders had already completed his run and knew the cattle. He spotted Jim's trouble. He rode over and commented dryly, "Jim, I like that two-spot brindle. She has bright eyes and hasn't been worked."

Jim tipped his hat in appreciation to the rider, who returned to his post. Cutters were like that. Although they were competitors in the same event, they wanted to see the other fellow have a fair shot.

That two-spot brindle was at the back of the herd near the rear fence. Jim wanted to go deep on his first cut anyway, so he decided to try for her. He walked Mary Jane across the time line, triggering the clock on their two and a half minutes, and eased her into the herd. The rider is in charge at this stage, and he carefully guided her through the cows toward the brindle. But

Bright Eyes was already aware of them and figured out they were up to no good. When Jim closed on her, she broke away from the fence, into the herd. Jim went after her anyway, but she slipped right past them, and they emerged from the herd with several cows scattering before them into the arena.

There was nothing to do but cut one of the scattered cows. He picked a fuzzy-tailed red to work, but a slick-coated red was right alongside her. Both cows were centered nicely in the arena, and the others had run back into the herd. Jim figured one of these would quickly peel off and return to the herd as well, so he dropped the reins to signal he was turning things over to his horse.

Now it was between Mary Jane and one of these cows. But he had figured wrong about the two reds. It was like somebody had glued them together. They broke into a hard run to the right, and Mary Jane went with them and cut them off. They reversed direction simultaneously, like choreographed dancers, and tried to slip past her left. Mary Jane was on top of that too and cut them off again. They returned to center arena to ponder the situation.

Both reds were hot, but a horse and rider can score no points until working a single cow. Jim was reluctant to quit such good cows, so he allowed Mary Jane to keep working them, hoping one would split off and get back to the herd. Meanwhile, the clock was running. Finally, the slick red saw an opening and shot back into the herd. But when Fuzzy Tail saw that and realized Mary Jane was not going to allow her to do the same, she lost heart and stopped trying. Jim raised the reins in disgust to signal he was quitting the cow.

He had burned over a minute on Fuzzy Tail and the slick red with nothing to show for it. There was 1:23 left on the clock, and he needed to give Pederson some action shots and show the judges some points. Despite the time pressure, he took a breath to compose himself and figure out his next move. A white-bellied blackie was on the edge of the herd and might be worth some quick points. He cut her out easily enough, and when he blocked her return, she positioned herself nicely a little off from center arena. Good enough. Jim dropped the reins.

Mary Jane wanted to play, but White Belly looked like she had already been worked. She took a couple of shots at getting back to the herd but appeared to know this was not going to work. You could not quit a cow without penalty unless she was moving away from the herd or had obviously stopped trying. Jim quit on her as soon as she turned away, with 0:58 left on the clock. If he did not give Pederson some good action shots on the next cow, he would not have enough points to advance to the next Go Round either, and that would be that.

Once again, Jim took a deep breath and studied the herd. That two-spot brindle was away from the fence now, and Jim figured a deep cut from behind might just nudge her loose. If she was any good, it was his best shot at getting back into the game. He quietly took Mary Jane through the cows at an angle that put them behind the brindle and then turned so she could nudge the little lady from behind. The startled brindle shot forward, and with Mary Jane behind, she popped right out of the herd. Jim had never seen such a clean pop, and the brindle looked mixed up about how in the world she had gotten to where she was. Jim quickly cut off her instinctive shot at streaking back to the herd. When that didn't work, she retreated to reconsider, and, to Jim's amazement, settled almost dead center in the arena to study the situation. Jim immediately positioned Mary Jane before her and dropped the reins.

The brindle was alert and intelligent and had bright eyes, all right. She and Mary Jane made eye contact and took each other's measure.

"Look out—here I come!" the brindle seemed to say.

"Oh, you think so?" Mary Jane's body language replied. Mary Jane had not had a good cow in quite some time, and the smell of this one made her ears pop up.

And man, did those two go at it. The brindle had more tricks than a gambler with a crooked deck and played every card. She tried to let Mary Jane go long on a lateral run so she could cut back inside, but the mare had her number and reversed right with her. The cow had some slick feints that could throw off a good horse on a bad day but not Mary Jane today. That cow dealt one card from the bottom of her funny deck after another. Mary Jane trumped each one and her stance said, "What else you got?" Folks in the stand began to catch fire too, hooting and whistling.

Now the brindle repositioned herself in center arena and got very snake-eyed, with her hind end up and tail waving, and seemed to say, "Okay, I'm done playing with you!"

And that was when Mary Jane did something Jim had never seen from her before. She got down almost to her knees, eyeball-to-eyeball with that cow, and seemed to say, "Are you talking to me? You want some more of me? Come and get it, Shorty!"

This faked out the brindle, and she broke off in another run, but Mary Jane cut her off easily. Then the buzzer sounded and it was over.

It was not a large crowd, but they were appreciative with whistles and applause. Ned had the pictures he wanted, and Jim was sure they had advanced to the next Go Round. They had scored a seventy-four and were well positioned to actually win.

But Lee was at the fence, waving to him. Jim rode over.

"We're good, Jimbo! You blew that lawyer's eyeballs out. He's executing the wire transfer now, and the Bakersfield fellow is here with his trailer. Bring Spooks around front so Pederson can sit on her for a few pictures, and we'll wrap this puppy."

"What about the next Go Round?"

"We're done here, Jimbo."

Jim was fired up about his run and disappointed to skip the next Go Round but knew Lee was right. The game was in the bag, and nothing was to be gained by pushing this. Mary Jane looked like the happiest mare in the world about what she had done, and Jim was feeling a lot better too. He did not see how anything could go wrong now.

CHAPTER 10

THREE-HORSE MONTE

Jim rode Mary Jane back through the warm-up pen to their trailers in the rear lot, rubbing and patting her neck the whole way and telling her what a fine, wonderful lady she was. When he dismounted, he threw his arms around her neck and hugged her in a rush of grateful emotion.

But there was little time. He slipped on a halter, tied her to the trailer, and pulled off the saddle. He set out some fresh water for her and hung a hay net from the trailer for her to nibble on. Then he threw the saddle on Spooks, bridled her, swung up into the saddle, and rode back to the arena.

Several men on horseback were settling fresh cows against the back fence for the next Go Round. Lee brought Pederson into the center arena so they could get some pictures of him with his new horse. Ned was still shaking with excitement over the pictures he had captured during the run when Jim rode up on Spooks.

"There she is!" Ned cried. "There's my horse!"

Jim dismounted, helped Pederson up into the saddle, and handed up his cowboy hat. Lee took a couple of pictures of Ned wearing Jim's hat and sitting on Spooks and a couple more with Ned waving the hat high in the air.

Then Jim helped Ned down from the horse, and the three of them walked Spooks out to the front of the arena. Josephson was waiting with his trailer to haul her to Dallas. Jim stripped the bridle and saddle and helped the man load Spooks. Ned contacted Walker in Switzerland on his phone and handed it to Lee. Walker confirmed the wire transfer had gone through, and Lee surrendered Lady Joe's papers to Pederson.

"Mr. Pederson, it's been a pleasure."

"Boys, you sure know how to show a fellow a good time," Ned told them. "I need to get back to Dallas with this champ and start throwing dinner parties. Don't worry about me anymore. Josephson here will drop me off at the airport."

"Well, you have a safe trip, then," Lee told him.

"Maybe I'll be out this way sometime when we don't have horses to deal with, and we can get into some real trouble." Ned winked at Lee. And the truck and trailer pulled onto the 101 headed south.

Jim and Lee watched until they disappeared from sight. Jim heaved a deep sigh. "Lee, please tell me it's over and I can start breathing again."

"It's better than over." Lee took his friend by the arm. "Walk with me, Jimbo. You need to hear what Walker just told me."

"Did he say he's bringing us into the horse business?"

They walked back toward the arena past parked trailers in the lot.

"Well, no, he didn't say that. In fact, he said he's been knocking back shots over me being in charge out here. But you know what? I told him about your seventy-four and how Pederson was so excited, he closed the deal without waiting for the second Go Round. Walker couldn't talk for about a minute. Then he said he was damned if he didn't make more money in the horse business by staying in Europe with me running things. He said it was going to be his first good night's sleep in a week, and he intends to pay us a commission."

"You mean money?"

"Five percent."

"That can't be right. Lee, that's twenty thousand dollars."

"Ten apiece. How about it, amigo? Not a bad start in the horse business."

"Oh, man. We can't take that."

"Why not?"

"Wake up, Lee. What we did is against the law! If we get caught, we could maybe plead stupidity. But if we profit from it, we could end up in the penitentiary."

"Nobody's going to the penitentiary, Jimbo. It's over. Spooks is going to live out a nice, easy life in Dallas entertaining Pederson's dinner guests. Walker got top dollar for Lady Joe's papers. That's how it is—and nobody is ever going to know any different."

Jim thought about it. "Well, I guess you can take your money, then. It's different with me."

"How are you different?"

"I'm a married man. It would reflect poorly on my wife."

"Wake up, compadre. Francine won't know either. Nobody will ever know."

"I'll know! I couldn't keep something like that from her. I swear to God there is not a more decent girl on this earth. I can't disrespect her by doing something like that. I just can't!"

Lee took his friend by the shoulders and positioned him against the side of a trailer. Lee pointed with two fingers at his own eyes. "Jimmy, I want you to look at me. Look me straight in the eyes and listen carefully." He paused for emphasis. "Francine might divorce you. Now, you said so yourself. What if she walks out? You'll be left with nothing and feel like a pretty damn big fool for passing up ten thousand dollars."

"Yesterday you said she wouldn't leave me."

"Forget what I said yesterday. Do not take advice about women from me. Hey, I could drive you down to Pasadena and let you talk to scientists at the Jet Propulsion Laboratory. Not even they can tell you what Francine is going to do."

Jim was shaking his head in bewilderment again. "I swear to God I just can't tell right from wrong anymore. I used to think it was easy to do the right thing. Now I'm all mixed up and just can't tell anymore."

"Take the money, Jimbo. Trust me, when you tell Francine you made ten thousand dollars off this deal, she's going to be real proud of you for once."

"I guess you're right."

"And forget the law. This thing is over."

They walked in silence.

About then Jim noticed that somebody was approaching them from behind across the lot. "Lee, tell me I'm wrong. That looks like the law coming for us right now."

Lee looked over his shoulder to see Sheriff Captain Arthur Briscom coming toward them. "That's just Art Briscom," he said. "He's a friend of my pop. He's not interested in us."

Briscom grinned and waved to them and walked faster.

"This sure didn't take long," Jim said. The boys stopped walking and waited for the sheriff to catch up to them.

"Let me do the talking," Lee said. "I'll shit around with him and see what he wants."

And then he was upon them. "Hello, boys." He greeted them cheerfully.

"Hey, Art. What's up?"

"Jim Harrison and Lee Estes! My goodness, haven't seen you fellows in a while. Thought I'd come say hello and see how everything's going."

"We're doing all right," Lee told him.

"Say, I was talking to your pop just yesterday. He says you're working on the Walker place."

"Few months now."

"I'm glad to hear that. How's it going, anyway?"

"It's going pretty well."

"Your pop says Walker's in Switzerland, and with the boys on the road, you've pretty much got the run of the place."

"Pretty much."

"Well, you made him proud for once. I called the ranch just now because I need to ask you something. They said I could find you here. This works out real good, because it saves me a trip to Ojai."

"Ask me what, exactly?"

"Well, I need your opinion about something. Come over here a minute. Tell me what you think."

Lee and Jim followed Briscom through the lot of parked trailers to a Sheriff Department vehicle. A horse trailer was hitched to it with a fine-looking blue roan mare inside.

"I want you to climb up there and look at that horse for me," Briscom said.

Lee and Jim stared at the trailer in awe. Lee did like the sheriff said and slowly climbed up the boards to peer inside for a closer look.

"Lee, if that is not Lady Joe," the sheriff said, "I will kiss your ass right here in the parking lot and give you ten minutes to draw a crowd."

Lee stepped down from the trailer and was very quiet for a minute. "Yes, sir, that's her," he finally admitted. He was white in the face and looked like he was going to pass out.

"She's not been reported missing or anything," Briscom commented dryly.

"Well, no, sir. I was too scared to do that," Lee admitted.

"Your pop told me yesterday that Walker has a buyer for this horse. Some fellow is flying out from Dallas to pick her up."

"Yes, sir, that's correct," Lee said. In fact, Ned had just pulled out of the lot with Spooks, but Lee figured this was close enough to the truth.

"What did you intend to do when the man showed up and you didn't have his horse?"

"Well, I've been sweating bullets about that part, sir."

"I'll bet you have!" Briscom said, shaking his head in a combination of disbelief and dismay.

Then, to the surprise of the boys, Briscom started laughing while still shaking his head in disbelief. He clapped a confident hand on Lee's shoulder and shook him reassuringly. "It's all right, son! I've got your horse back for you. You don't have to worry anymore."

Lee was still in a daze. "Sheriff, I looked to hell and gone for this animal. Where did you find her?"

"Why, I saw her on the television news this morning, prancing down the middle of the 101 interstate. It was a blue roan mare nobody had reported missing. Well, after talking to your pop yesterday, I knew you were working for the Walker outfit, so it didn't take much to put two and two together. I said to myself, 'Good God, Lee Estes has lost Lady Joe!'"

Briscom slipped into another fit of laughter and started turning red in the face but then got a hold of himself again.

"I'm sorry, Lee." He chuckled and waved his hand. "Give me a minute here." He finally calmed down enough to talk but was still shaking his head. "Anyway, me and your pop go back a long ways. I knew how proud he was of you working for Walker, so I hitched up a trailer and hurried out there before Animal Control arrived. I took possession of her on behalf of the county and told highway patrol I knew the owner and would return her."

"Sheriff, I sure do appreciate that," Lee said weakly, still very pale and bewildered.

Briscom gripped him reassuringly by the shoulder again. "Here's the thing, son," he said. "Nobody knows about this but you, me, and Jim. Your pop would have a heart attack if he found out. What I'm going to do is unhitch this trailer and leave her with you. Go sneak her back on the ranch and return the trailer when you get around to it. Your pop is a good man, Lee. I want him to be real proud of you for once."

"Yes, sir. I sure do appreciate this, Sheriff."

"Jim, it's good to see you again," Briscom said. "Anyway, I need to get back on duty, so I'll leave you boys to take it from here."

Briscom unhitched the trailer and drove off. Jim and Lee stood in the lot, looking at it. Lee climbed up the side to look at the mare again. She was pretty and proud.

"Is that Lady Joe, sure enough?" Jim asked.

"It's her." Lee dropped back to the pavement and dusted off his hands.

"Where does this leave us, exactly?"

"Well, we got an extra horse, Jimbo."

"I see that. What do we do about it?"

Lee considered the possibilities. "I sure can't take her back to the ranch. Walker collected four hundred big ones for her, and anyway, her papers are on the way to Dallas."

Lady Joe

"We have an extra stall at home, but I couldn't bring her there either," Jim said. "There's no way I could explain this to Francine."

"No, I can't think of a story we could sell her," Lee admitted.

The boys pondered this further in silence. Lee broke into a cold sweat. "Jimbo, we need to shoot this horse."

"Hey! No way, partner! I'm no horse shooter!"

"Me neither, but think about it! This horse could put us in the penitentiary."

"I don't care how far back in a cell they throw us. Nobody is shooting this horse. I won't, and I'll shoot you before I let you do it."

"You're not thinking this through, compadre. Newspapers will have our pictures all over the front page. Francine will be hiding her face and running from reporters. She'll line up those horse lawyers she works for and divorce your sorry ass from here to San Antonio. Is that what you want?"

"We still have to think of something else."

"I'm all ears, amigo. If you've got a better idea, now would be the time to share it."

They fell into deep silence, sulking around the trailer. Neither of them could come up with anything.

"It's getting late," Lee said. "Francine is going to expect you back with Mary Jane before long."

Jim had been sitting on the trailer stem in deep thought, and now something came to him. Slowly, he rose to his feet and drew a set of papers from his pocket. He studied them.

"What are you looking at?"

"Spooks's papers." Jim was thinking aloud. "Here's how we do this. We run Lady Joe up to Salinas or some-place where nobody knows us. We'll book her in a board-ing ranch up there as Spooks."

Lee took the papers from him and looked them over. "I guess it would work." He frowned skeptically. "But what then?"

"That's it."

"Do you have any idea how much this would cost? Boarding, feed, farrier, vet bills."

"We pay it."

"Every month?"

"Until we think of something else."

"That's almost like alimony."

"Walker's giving us a commission, isn't he? Well, easy come, easy go."

Lee pondered this carefully. He could not find a flaw in Jim's proposal. In fact, as he scrutinized the papers, he began to see even greater possibilities.

"Holy bat shit," he whispered in awe. He leaped up onto the trailer again with the papers in hand and looked at Lady Joe. "Jimbo, get up here."

Jim climbed up alongside him to see what Lee was talking about.

"It's been, what, four, five years since anybody's showed her?"

"I guess so."

"We can take Lady Joe on the road with these papers."

"What? Ride her as Spooks?"

"Hey, we're outlaws now, Jimbo. It's like you said. There's no escaping that part. Seems to me if a man goes bad, he should at least make money at it."

"You're serious. You want to enter her in events?"

"You ride her. I'll pick cows. No, think about this. I'll tell you exactly how it's going to go. Word will get around that Lee Estes and Jim Harrison are haulin' some no-name nag that Lee bought off a fellow in Hollister for two hundred and fifty dollars. Everybody's going to be laughing their butts off at us. But you know what? You and me, Jimbo. They won't laugh long, because we're going to shove this no-name nag right up their asses."

Jim was dazed by the boldness of the scheme. Never in his wildest dreams had he imagined he would end up a criminal living outside the law. And yet for the life of him, he did not see how he could escape that fate.

Lee dropped down from the trailer to the ground. "This is how I see things. Our backs are against the wall with this horse, however you look at it. If we can't shoot her, let's haul her. We can do this!"

"How will I explain it to Francine?"

"Let me talk to her. I'll say Pederson decided to buy Lady Joe instead, but it looks like Spooks isn't such a bad cutter after all, and we want to try her out on the road. We're investing our commission from Walker in a shot at making a name for ourselves in the horse business. She'll buy that, won't she?"

Jim did not say anything. Lee noticed that he was still up on the trailer, head buried in his arms, standing very still.

"Hey, are you asleep up there, partner?"

"Leave me alone," Jim said. "Thinking is too hard. I need to rest my mind for a while."

CHAPTER 11

FELONY HAULIN'

And so began what Lee and Jim were to forever look back on as the year of felony hauling.

Jim had a long talk with Francine, and they agreed his career at the restaurant was going nowhere. She knew where her husband's heart was and said he should use the Walker money to go on the road with Lee and show the new mare they were so excited about. Secretly Francine believed year's end would find Jim broke and without a job, but she resolved not to think about that until the moment was upon her. She would make a decision about their future at that time.

Walker was so pleased with Lee that he gave him a year's leave to go on the road and even loaned them a truck and trailer. Lee took the liberty of painting a logo on the truck doors:

Harrison & Lee
Cow Cutters

Lee also persuaded Sally Temple to quit her job as waitress and join the team to help with the driving and share in the many chores. Jim personally looked after Lady Joe to make sure she was comfortable and safe. But there was a lot more to going on the road: vehicle maintenance, motel reservations, laundry, buying groceries, and pitching in as needed to keep them organized and on schedule. For this, Lee offered Sally a salary out of his commission money. She was tired of restaurant customers complaining about undercooked eggs or propositioning her and then not leaving a tip when she told them where to stick it. She jumped at the opportunity to take to the road and work horses.

Lady Joe was not a legend but was well remembered as a strong horse that almost always placed in the money, and with a good cow in front of her, she could put the contest out of reach. Walker had a lot of affection for her, but because he had so many promising younger horses to take on the road, he had rewarded her with early retirement, and she had not worked cows for several years. Jim needed to find out if they still interested her. If they did, he was confident she would shut them down.

Lady Joe did not know Jim and was a little wary of him at first. She had been through a lot recently: spooked by a mule deer, lost in the foothills of the coastal mountains, the confusion of an interstate traffic jam, and now this strange man who wanted into her life. She tested him for a while, but Jim promptly and firmly corrected her when she misbehaved. He looked to be all right. Then he put a few good cows in front of her at a weekend cutting. That was when she became confident that he knew what he was doing. She sensed that this would work and began to trust that nothing bad would happen if she followed his lead. From there, affection between them began to grow.

They started out slow with a few local cuttings in California and up the Pacific Coast. Jim still had a lot to learn about Lady Joe: how much of a warm-up she needed, how she rode on hard ground arenas compared to soft ground ones, whether she was chargey with a cow or stood her ground, how well she responded to leg pressure, and all the other little things. She was an older horse now, no longer the powerful and alert three-year-old of the futurity year in which she had placed fifth. But she still had plenty of cow in her, and Jim had whetted her appetite.

That spring, they took to the road in what was to be a crazy year. Lee and Sally impulsively married in Reno in July, got divorced two months later by taking a round-trip air flight to Tijuana, and then married again that October in Oklahoma City.

Lady Joe showed real interest in returning to competition from the start. She won her first two Non-Pro events in Sacramento and Fresno with a 219 and 216 respectively (these being sum total scores of three judges at the contests). They placed several times before winning yet again at Los Gatos with a 228. Though the events were not well attended, even nationally the cutting world is a small and close-knit family, and across country people began to sense a change in the weather. Nobody had ever heard of Jim Harrison or Lee Estes, and Spooks was an older horse with zero earnings that had not been on anybody's radar. Clearly, something unusual was afoot.

And yet it all checked out. Lee and Jim were from San Luis Obispo, where they had attended cuttings in high school. Rancher Chuck Freehling of Hollister confirmed to the *Daily Chatter*: "Yes, I sold Spooks to Lee Estes for two hundred and fifty dollars, and I'll tell you why. I am a goddamn fool. My whole life, I've blowed every shot at the big time straight down a rat hole. This is no different. I had not even heard of cutting and still could not tell you what it is exactly. Spooks was an all right horse but nothing special that I could see. I put her on Craigslist for two hundred and fifty dollars. Lee Estes showed up with fire shooting out of his ass, saying he needed her right away. Seemed like to me at the time something was funny about that, and now I see why he wanted her so bad."

Jim called Francine from the road each night to tell her how the day went and whether they were hauling or had competed that day.

"It sounds like Lee found a pretty good horse," she admitted. "Don't get too excited though. Just stay focused and keep doing what you're doing. You were always the best cutter of the three of us, but that's an older horse, and you have a long way to go yet."

They finally moved east with another win at Reno with a 222. Legendary horse trainer Teddy Abbot caught up with them just as they were about to pull out of the lot. Teddy had risen to oversee the personal ranch holdings of reclusive billionaire Charles Robert Scoggins, a position that made him a major player in the horse world. Lee and Sally had just gotten married for the first time and were misbehaving in the shotgun seat when Teddy flagged them down. Jim slid out of the truck to talk to him.

"Mr. Abbot, no need to introduce yourself. It's a real pleasure to meet you," he said. "I'm Jim, and that's Lee up there. He just got married, so you need to excuse those two." Lee and his new wife quickly got serious when they realized who had pulled them over.

"Jim, I'd like to look at Spooks, if it's all right with you," Teddy said.

"Sure enough, Mr. Abbot."

The trainer crawled up on the trailer and looked her over. "Yes, she's older now and looks a little different, but I had this horse when she was a filly."

He dropped down from the trailer and explained. "We go through a lot of young horses at the Scoggins operation, finding what each one is best suited for and how to train them. Those with a lot of cow in them become cutters. Others might be fit for rodeo, ranch, and other talents. I was just starting out with the Scoggins people back then and remember working with Spooks. My judgment was that she was amiable enough but without any special abilities. It didn't look to me worth the time to spend on her in any of the disciplines we covered. I'm surprised you've made such a good cutting horse out of her."

"Well, we don't have much money and went with the only horse we could afford."

"Mr. Scoggins is impressed with what you've done with her. I thought you'd like to know he has his eye on you." Teddy Abbott thanked them for their time, wished them luck, and took his leave.

Though it was a thrill to hear that Teddy Abbot and Charles Scoggins had taken notice of them, for Jim there was also something foreboding about it. They were starting to get the attention of important horse people, as they had schemed, but it seemed to Jim that eventually one of these same experts would figure out he was riding Lady Joe. He felt that shoe ready to drop at every venue, and should it fall their fame would instantly transform to notoriety and disgrace. The trick was to know how far to push this before quitting the road.

"It's been five, six years at least since anybody showed her," Lee kept reminding him. But Jim could not bear to imagine what Francine would think if they got caught. Sally didn't know what they were doing either, but that did not bother Lee.

"I'm cheating on my wife, Lee," Jim confessed in a moment of abysmal despair.

"What are you talking about, Jimbo?"

"I didn't tell her the truth about this."

"You didn't lie to her, either. I'm the one who made up a story."

"Well, I'd hate to have her find out about this on the television news."

"Jimbo, you need to stop trying to figure stuff out. The world is a crazy place. Neither of us ever dreamed of this kind of opportunity. We won't see another shot like this in a hundred years. Let's just do it. We can go to hell together if it comes to that."

Lee was not especially reassuring, but Jim could see little alternative now that they were committed. Besides, he and Lady Joe had taken a genuine liking to each other and were working better together each day, and Jim was loving every minute of it. The only thing to do, he figured, was to stay focused on what was in front of him.

When they pushed further east toward Texas, the competition got tougher, but the novelty of who they were and what they were doing with an unknown horse continued generating interest and new followers.

"Who Zat?" was the title of a *Daily Chatter* post about the Cinderella story of these young horsemen.

"Which one of you found him?" asked the *Chatter* reporter at Will Rogers Coliseum in Fort Worth.

"I did," Lee said, stepping forward with an arm around his new wife. "But I lost her shooting pool to Jim."

"That's one hell of a story."

"No, that's just Lee Estes," Sally said, pinching her husband in the ribs. "He does stuff like that all the time."

That afternoon, Jim and Lady Joe placed fourth with a 213, as they doggedly continued accumulating points on the road.

One day, Francine was working at her desk in the law office when a senior partner, Eric Longtree, approached with an important new client. "Mr. Lassiter," he said, "I want you to meet Jim Harrison's wife. She's one of our paralegals."

Francine's mind spun at the introduction, and she was so flustered that she almost stumbled as she rose to her feet and offered her hand.

"I'm Francine," she managed to say.

"Mrs. Harrison, this is a real pleasure," Lassiter replied warmly, taking her hand in a firm grip. "You must be awfully proud of your husband these days."

"Yes, he's doing really well so far."

"How did the two of you meet, if you don't mind my asking?"

"We used to go to cuttings together in high school."

"So he married his high school sweetheart. My goodness, what a wonderful story! I'll have to tell my wife about this."

Subsequently, Francine came to understand that she was expected to attend the firm's country club social gatherings to mix with clients. If Jim was in town and available, she was to persuade him to accompany her.

The following week, Lady Joe took on a cow from some other planet to win at South Point with a 231. "Jim Harrison on Spooks" was the cover of *Quarter Horse News.* The story about the three of them on the road was a little confusing, because it said Lee and Sally were newlyweds when in fact they had just divorced in Mexico, and by the time that was corrected in a later issue, they had already remarried again.

But the focus of the feature was how these young people had taken to the road with an older horse purchased for two hundred and fifty dollars and were shaking up the Non-Pro circuit like poker dice in a craps game.

"I'd given up on cutting," one horseman admitted to a reporter. "To be honest, I just got tired of losing. I work for a living and can't afford a trained cutting horse. I figured you had to be rich to win at these things. Well, Jim Harrison has proven me wrong. I intend to get back in the arena with the horse I've got and if nothing else scare a few cows."

Jim was described as a sincere and soft-spoken young man with an uncanny sensitivity for how his horse was thinking and what a cow was likely to do. He attributed his success to his wife. "She told me to quit my job and go on the road with some money I came into," he said. "Otherwise I wouldn't be here. She's still at home, working and paying the bills. I feel bad about that and want to keep doing well on the road to justify her faith in me."

Lee and Sally were presented as a lively young couple who knew how to have a good time but were also old friends and experienced cutters and cow pickers who provided Jim a solid support team on the road. "I couldn't do this without them," he said.

The next morning, Francine found a stack of Jim's issue of *Quarter Horse News* on her desk, along with a list of important clients. She was asked to prevail upon her husband to autograph a copy personally to each client. She was a little annoyed and embarrassed about the attention he was getting but at the same time felt guilty because she realized how unfair those feelings were to Jim. He was her husband and merely doing what she had been so aggravated with him for not doing for so long. He was finally showing his potential and making something of himself.

At Francine's request—made under duress from Mr. Longtree—Jim flew home to attend a county club social for the firm's clients with her. Jim was shy and soft-spoken and looked uncomfortable in a suit and necktie, mingling with such important guests. But to Francine's amazement, he was the hit of the evening. Nobody asked him about Middle East politics or the wisdom of current Federal Reserve fiscal policy. They wanted to know what it feels like on the hurricane deck of a cutting horse when she gets down in front of a cow.

"It is the best seat in the house," he told them. "What is it like? Well, the world and all its troubles go away. There's nothing left but you, the horse, and that cow. All you have to worry about for two and a half minutes is what's in that box."

One client confided to Jim that he had done some cutting in younger years and once considered a career in the horse industry. "Between work and family, those ideas got lost somehow. But after seeing what you've accomplished with that mare, I've started looking around for a good cutting horse. I am blessed with financial success, but a man only needs so much money. I had forgotten how it feels after a good run on a cutting horse."

"I'd forgotten that feeling too," Jim admitted. "Fortunately for me, an opportunity came along, and I took it. You can afford to make your own opportunity, and the right horse is out there for you somewhere, so I hope you pursue this." The client shook his hand and thanked him for the encouragement.

Another client said he had been thinking of selling his ranch because neither of his sons nor his daughter had ever shown an interest in it. They were around Jim's age and had followed Jim's adventures with Lee, Sally, and Spooks over the past year. Now they were enthusiastic about cutting and intended to try their own luck on the road. His wife had been saying for years that they should sell the place, because the children would rather have the money, but now it looked like it would stay in the family after all. The client said he drove up from Santa Barbara that night to shake Jim's hand and thank him personally.

Jim and Francine were young, attractive, and unpretentious. They were the surprise hit of the evening. When Eric Longtree proposed a toast to the young cutter, Jim pulled his wife alongside to share it with him.

Francine was strangely quiet on the drive home.

"I was very impressed with you tonight, sir," she said when they got back to the house.

"I was pretty nervous about doing this," he admitted. "But everybody made me feel like I belonged there. I didn't expect to like them, but I did." He shed the necktie and jacket and looked for a beer in the refrigerator, without luck.

"Since taking Spooks on the road with Lee, you've become a lot more sure of yourself. I never saw that coming."

Jim did not understand the remark. She looked a little nervous.

"Never saw what coming?"

"Probably you meet a lot of girls out there," she added. "I wouldn't blame you if you left me for one of them after the way I've treated you."

She wondered for a moment if she had lost him.

Jim swept up his wife in his arms so quickly that she cried out in surprise. He carried her into the bedroom and plopped her on their bed.

"What's happening?" she asked with a sparkle in her eyes.

"I brought home the prettiest girl at the country club," he said. "Do you know what's going to happen next?"

"What?"

"I'm going to take off every stitch of your clothes."

"You sound pretty sure of yourself, cowboy."

"You don't think it'll happen?"

"Try your luck and see."

He did, and that night they got started on a family.

On an overcast morning in the late fall, billionaire Scoggins's overseer, Teddy Abbot, knocked on the door of Jim's motel room somewhere near Houston. Jim had been riding the day before and was sleepy but realized the moment he saw Abbot that it was about something important.

"Jim, we need to talk."

"Do you want to come inside?"

"No, why don't you put some clothes on? Let's take a walk."

Jim got dressed, and they went down the stairs past the swimming pool and walked in silence for a while across the weed-covered lot behind the motel.

"Mr. Scoggins needs you to stop showing Lady Joe," Teddy said.

That shoe Jim had been afraid of finally dropped. He had not expected Teddy Abbot would be the one to drop it.

"What did he say, exactly?" Jim asked quietly.

"This shit has to stop."

Jim nodded. "How many people know?"

"Just me and the old man. He took an interest in you early on and told me to see what was going on. I used to own Spooks and spotted Lady Joe right away."

"Why didn't you say something then?"

"Mr. Scoggins was all right with it at first, because he said what you were doing was good for the horses. You've been getting a lot of young people your age interested in them. But if it goes on much longer, somebody is going to figure it out, and a scandal like that would be bad for the horses. He's concerned about the horses. He could care squat what anybody else thinks about this."

"What happens to me and Lee?"

"He wants you fellas to come see him at his ranch. He says you need to hammer some things out."

"Hammer what out? What does that mean?"

"He didn't explain that part."

CHAPTER 12
THE HORSES

The spread Charles Robert Scoggins had chosen for his homestead was a little north of Santa Barbara. It is spectacular country, where the San Andreas shoved alluvial topsoil into anticline folds, which nature then sculpted into gently rolling golden hills. Scoggins said God was so pleased about this that he studded the hills with an occasional oak tree so riders could rest in the shade. There is no finer horse county anywhere on earth.

The main house was a single level built in Mediterranean style, with several guest residences joined by garden pathways. For the entertainment of guests, he had a polo field, tennis courts, and a swimming pool with a bathhouse. Though Scoggins had not entertained guests for many years now, a full-time staff maintained

these facilities, which always looked as if they had been
built yesterday.

The property was a fully operational horse ranch
with two barns of thirty-six stables each, an enclosed
arena with warm-up pen, and several round pen cor-
rals for working horses. The ranch did no breeding but
purchased young two-year-old horses to be broken and
trained in a discipline appropriate to their abilities and
then sold them for profit. Hands on horseback worked
a few hundred head of cattle. Though the ranch was
rarely profitable, the old man enjoyed watching younger generations of men and women working his livestock
and training the two-year-olds.

Scoggins lived alone in the big house and for some
years had lost interest in meeting anybody he did not already know. A visit from an old acquaintance was always
a welcome event. His children had long since grown
up and moved away and had given him grandchildren
that he rarely saw. The two wives who divorced him had
retired elsewhere with their settlement money, one to
the south of France and the other somewhere in the
Caribbean. He heard little from them except in regard
to trivial matters. Sometimes he allowed himself to re-
call the fun times with them in younger days. He would
also think about the girls of his youth who had broken
his heart and made a clean getaway. He wondered what
had become of them and whether they had done better
or worse for themselves by that. But mostly he whiled

away his days exploring the ranch on horseback or resting under an oak on a lazy afternoon, contemplating the potential of his latest crop of two-year-olds.

Jim had returned to California with Lady Joe, as instructed by Teddy Abbot. People speculated about his abrupt withdrawal from the Non-Pro circuit, but he was told not to comment on that. Only Jim and Lee knew what was afoot; their wives had no more clue about the Lady Joe fraud than the rest of the Non-Pro circuit.

He received further instructions when Jim and Lee were summoned to the Santa Barbara ranch. Because this might require several days, Mr. Scoggins told the boys to bring their wives along. The ladies were to pack bathing suits, tennis rackets, riding tack, and anything else that interested them. They were the first officially invited guests of the ranch in many years.

It was unclear to Jim if this last part was a good or bad thing. Only the ladies were invited. Jim and Lee were summoned. They envied the blissful ignorance of their wives.

Whatever was afoot, the significance of the invitations was not lost on the girls. They knew the official Scoggins invitations on formal guest cards had not been seen in many years. They confirmed in a heartbeat.

When Francine showed hers to the senior partners at the law firm, they were skeptical. These cards were collectors' items from years past and were occasionally auctioned off at estate sales. But skepticism gave way

to greed and the remote possibility of someday repre-
senting Scoggins. They insisted Francine take time off
with pay and gave her a supply of business cards to pass
around. She thought the latter embarrassing and tacky
but solemnly promised to do so. Though she was usually
meticulously honest, she conveniently forgot to bring
them with her.

Francine was the only one of the foursome who
owned a car, so she drove them to the ranch. The property dwarfed the Walker spread and anything else they
had seen. The main house, several miles past the entrance gate, was not even visible from the road. They
drove past a frog pond, a man longing a horse in a
round pen, and eventually the horse barns before the
residence finally came in sight.

Teddy Abbot was waiting with the house staff when
they pulled up. The staff quickly and efficiently unloaded luggage and whisked away Francine's car. Teddy told
the girls that the staff was at their disposal, and after
they had settled in, they were free to do as they wished.

He took the boys by golf cart to one of the horse
barns, where stable hands had prepared three saddle
horses. They had time before meeting with Scoggins,
so Teddy showed them a little of the property. The girls
were already sunning themselves poolside as they set
out and waved to them.

Teddy displayed an obvious pride in the sprawling
land and facilities entrusted to his care but otherwise

played his cards close to the vest. He shared no anec-
dotes or personal intimacy. Neither Jim nor Lee could
sense whether he was merely a gracious host or was pre-
paring to hit them with something.

At the appointed time, he took them up one of those
golden rolling hills where the old man was resting under an oak on what appeared to be a lawn chair from
the swimming pool. That and a cheap folding card table
alongside it were weathered and appeared to be perma-
nent fixtures under his favorite tree. Scoggins's horse
grazed nearby, untethered. A pitcher of cold lemonade
and some sandwiches were on the card table. The view
of rolling country from there was dazzling.

The old man appeared deep in sleep under his hat
when they pulled up on the horses. Teddy dismounted
and nodded for the boys to do the same.

"Mr. Scoggins," he said softly, "I have a couple fellows
here to see you."

Scoggins lay silent a moment. Slowly, he pushed up
his hat and studied the boys. He had been dozing but
not asleep. The man was somewhere in his early eight-
ies, weathered but only slightly stooped and mentally
still very much of this world. He took his time getting
to his feet and then poured himself lemonade. Once he
was good and ready, he walked over and looked them
over. Jim and Lee removed their hats politely.

"You're Jim." He nodded toward Jim. "I guess you
must be Lee Estes. I've heard about you too."

"Yes, sir," Jim answered respectfully.

For once in his life, Lee was too terrified to say anything. He sensed that Scoggins was a man like his pop who could not be hustled with fast talk. Such situations left him with little to say.

"Are the ladies settled in?"

"Yes, sir. They were real pleased with the invitations."

"I asked Teddy to show you around the place a little."

"Yes, it's quite a setup you've got here," Jim said.

"We're fattening up some real nice reds down in south pasture. Did he show them to you?"

"No, sir, we didn't get that far."

"They're real pretty." He paused. "Well then." He was ready for the matter at hand.

Teddy Abbot mounted up. "I'll leave you fellows to talk," he said, and moved off down the hill.

Scoggins looked the boys over from head to foot. Eventually he shook his head, more in wonder and dismay than anything else. "I have to say this much. You fellas are the craziest sons of bitches I ever heard of in my life. The reason I asked you here was because I needed to see this for myself."

Jim did not say anything, and Lee was not about to.

"When Teddy told me somebody was tearing up the Non-Pro circuit with a mare we had quit on, I had him look into it. I have no idea in the world how you fellows pulled this off. Somehow, there's a lawyer in Dallas entertaining dinner guests with Spooks under Lady Joe's papers. Do I have that part right?"

"Yes, sir, that's correct. We didn't intend that exactly but couldn't get out of it somehow." Jim spoke quietly but clearly. There was no point in lying.

Scoggins studied Jim carefully. He took pride in his judgment of character, and for the life of him he read the young man to be sincere. "Well, Jim, you're a good cutter, I'll give you that. I suppose you boys must like the horses quite a bit."

"Yes, sir, we do, but they're expensive, and we couldn't do much about it. We never got anywhere near this far with them before."

Scoggins thought about that for a moment. "Jim, let me tell you the saddest story I know. I'm rich and you're crazy, and between us we might be the only two kinds of friend the horse has left."

Jim did not understand him, and Lee could not think of anything to say.

Scoggins tossed his lemonade out into the grass and set the paper cup upside down on the card table. He looked out across his fine, rolling hills. "Young people today aren't like what they used to be," he remarked thoughtfully. "They like their gadgets. It used to be if a young man wasn't talking about the girls, he was talking about horses. People once talked about them as casually as they talked about the weather. Horses were just everywhere you see, and a man could scarcely get through the day without one. I believe pants were invented by a fellow who got tired of riding on his nuts under a robe."

The boys did not say anything. The old man was still gazing off at the hills as he warmed to the subject, and Jim began to wonder if he had forgotten they were there. "Horses plowed the fields, helped gather the harvest, and delivered the crops to the cities," Scoggins said. "If you needed to be somewhere, the horse would get you there. If you wanted something delivered, the horse would haul it in a wagon. It was as necessary to everyday life as food and shelter, and it made civilization possible.

"When wars broke out, more horses got killed than people. I will not tell you what happened to British horses in the Crimean War. But Abner Doubleday saw a team pull an artillery piece into position at Gettysburg while they were being shot to pieces by Rebel infantry. Bullets ripped into them, but they didn't panic or quit until the gun was in place and only then dropped dead. A gunner loaded canister into the piece they had placed and blew away the Rebel infantry and held the position. War Department records say we lost six hundred thousand men in the Civil War and over a million horses and mules.

"Things went on like that for three thousand years until the invention of the internal combustion engine. When the Great War broke out in 1914, the whole world saw that one truck had more horsepower and could do more work than a whole team of horses. By the time the war ended, a lot of people had stopped talking about horses.

"What they liked about the automobile was that if you turned off the ignition, it stopped burning fuel. The horse will eat just as much if you ride it or not, because its motor is always running. Wealthy people began converting their stables into garages and trading their horses for automobiles. The grooms who had looked after horses learned how to drive and became chauffeurs.

"That's when people realized how much they had hated horses. Half their lives had been spent feeding or caring for them, mucking out stalls, and running up vet and farrier bills. All a car needed was a can of oil and a little gas. The city didn't need to hire street sweepers to keep manure off the roads, and that saved tax dollars too, you see."

The old man turn away from the hills, took a cigar from his pocket, and peeled off the wrapper. He returned to the card table to look for some matches.

"Say, would you fellas like a lemonade?"

The boys were too concerned with what Scoggins intended to do with them to care about refreshments. "No sir, I'm fine," Jim said. "Unless Lee wants any."

"I'm good too, but thank you," Lee added.

"Well, it's right here if you change your mind."

Scoggins lit the cigar, took a couple puffs to get it going, and then turned to face the boys. "Most people couldn't afford a motor car at first," he said. "Then

Henry Ford invented the Model T. He put the auto-mobile within reach of the common man. And that's when the great slaughter began." He spoke without a trace of emotion. "It was the most spectacular mas-sacre of horseflesh in human history. Nobody wanted them anymore. Prices collapsed to where you could not give a horse away or even pay a man to take one. Abandoned horses starved in the countryside and be-came a public nuisance. All across this country and Europe, people in cities, small towns, and villages dumped horses on slaughterhouses by the millions. They knocked them in the head with sledgehammers and ground them into hamburger and dog food. Look at pictures of New York or Chicago starting around 1870 and see what I'm talking about. Streets were filled with horses then, but by 1930 they were all gone.

"After three thousand years of service and sacrifice, in the blink of an eye, the horse had become a useless animal. It is too lean to raise for meat and too expensive to keep for companionship like a dog or cat. Many ex-perts predicted it would go extinct."

He paused for another puff on the cigar and gath-ered his thoughts. "I believe the horse survived because two kinds of people admired its natural beauty enough to save it. First, there were the rich like me who could afford to keep them as playthings, but there weren't nearly enough of us.

"It was the crazy ones who saved the horse. I'm talking about people who didn't have nearly the time or money to work with them and had no business throwing away their lives on horses, but they did it anyway because they fell in love with the animal and couldn't live without its companionship. What they did went against self-interest and common sense and deprived them of the opportunity to live a normal life, but they did it anyway. Many could not afford to buy a car, and they often had to work two jobs, but some way or another their horses always got fed and looked after. What can you say about people like that? I believe there are more crazy people than rich people, and the rich need to help out the crazy ones where they can."

Scoggins studied the two young men before him and then began to put out the cigar with his fingers.

"Which brings us to the problem at hand," he said. "Truth be told, at the end of the day, I don't much have an opinion one way or another about the breeders, organizations, and competitions. I'm for them to the degree they are good for the horse, but they lose me the minute they cross that line. The horse has had a long run in history, but its luck has about run out."

He turned and set the extinguished cigar carefully on the card table.

"That's why I took notice when a couple fellows that nobody had heard of came out of nowhere and started running up statistics on a horse nobody had heard of. It was a good story, generated a lot of interest, and brought some people back into the game who had quit."

Scoggins laughed a little and shook his head. "I have to say you shook up a few people in the industry pretty good there for a while. Well, I don't see where any harm has come of it. The price of cutting horses is up. That can't be a bad thing. I understand people who never heard of cutting are looking into it now because of you. We have young folks who never sat on a horse before showing up at events to see what it's all about."

"Well sir, we didn't know about any of that," Jim said. "We were just doing the best we could on the road."

"The thing is it looks to me like you've done a little too good. This has gone about as far as it can go before somebody figures it out. You fellows look all right to me, and I like what you're doing, but I can't let you get caught at it because of the horses, you see."

"We'll take her off the road, like you said."

"Well, here's the trouble, Jim. You can't just quit, because then everybody will wonder about that too. We don't want somebody looking into this."

"We might be in a bit of a fix, then," Lee said.

"I've given it some thought," Scoggins said. "Here's how this is going to work. Jim, Lee—I'm going to buy Lady Joe from you under Spooks's papers. Don't worry. You'll see a real nice price. That will explain why you're pulling Spooks off the road. I'll put Lady Joe to pasture out here as Spooks, just like that Dallas lawyer has

Spooks to pasture as Lady Joe. Both horses will have a good retirement."

Jim and Lee could scarcely believe what they were hearing. The old man intended to bail them out.

"Boys, here's my condition. The way I see it, the money you won on the road needs to go to a good horse charity. It's not like you cheated in the arena or anything, because anybody will admit you are real fine horsemen. The trouble is, Jim rode that horse under the wrong papers. So how about we give the prize money back to the horses and call it a wash? Are we on the same page so far?"

"Yes, sir, we're on the same page." Jim nodded.

"I'm not. Why should we give up our winnings?" Lee protested.

"Lee, we're getting money for the damn horse. Leave it alone."

Lee withered under Jim's stare. "Okay, I'm on the same page as Jim."

"That's good," the old man said. "We could leave it at this and walk away from the table."

"Yes, sir, we're more than willing to do that." Jim was hugely relieved that Francine would never learn the truth about this.

"Well, we're not quite done yet." The old man had clearly taken a liking to Jim and was willing to put up with Lee. "Here's the thing," he observed. "You fellows are the craziest sons of bitches I ever saw. If I let you walk away from here, you'll probably put the money I'm giving you into the horse business."

"Yes, sir, we were thinking somewhere along those lines," Jim admitted.

"Well, you don't want to do that, son. Listen to me. The only way anybody ever walked away with a million dollars in the horse business was by starting out with two million. I don't want you to put that money into horses. Keep it for your wives and families, because they're going to need it someday. That said, I do believe you ought to be in the business."

Jim and Lee looked at each other. They had no idea where the old man was going.

"I believe horses need more fellows like you in the industry to look out for them. But it's a serious commitment that you need to discuss with your wives, because it won't work if the ladies don't want to go along with it. That's why I had you bring them here. I want you to enjoy the facilities with them for a few days and talk this through. Decide where you want to be in the industry and come up with a business plan and some numbers. When you're ready with that, I want you to apply to the Scoggins Institute for a grant."

"The Institute does that?" Jim looked surprised.

"Well, no, they don't, but they will if I talk to them."

"I never heard of the Scoggins Institute having anything to do with horses," Lee said.

"We've been known to work with crazy people on occasion, though."

The boys looked at him. Scoggins's face showed the faint trace of a smile.

"It's time for you fellows to go join your wives," he said. "Stay as long as you like. You probably won't see much of me again, but when you apply to the Institute, I'll see that it works out. Anything else?"

"Well, sir, my mind is a flat blank right now," Jim admitted. "I need to let this sink in. But I sure would like to do this if I can bring my wife around."

"Well, mine will jump at the chance to not ever have to wait on tables again," Lee said. "I'm pretty sure she'll help me and Jim talk Francine out of becoming a horse lawyer."

Scoggins laughed. "Well, good luck with the ladies, then."

"It's been a real pleasure, Mr. Scoggins," Jim said.

"Mine too, boys."

Lee and Jim went to mount their horses.

"Jim, come back here a minute," the old man called.

Jim took his foot from a stirrup and went to see what he wanted. The old man shook his hand.

"Call me Charlie," he said.

Made in the USA
Middletown, DE
02 June 2018